Forever Fallen

by
Rick Wilson

authorHOUSE™

1663 LIBERTY DRIVE, SUITE 200
BLOOMINGTON, INDIANA 47403
(800) 839-8640
WWW.AUTHORHOUSE.COM

First published by AuthorHouse 07/19/05

ISBN: 1-4208-5439-9 (sc)

Printed in the United States of America
Bloomington, Indiana

This book is printed on acid-free paper.

For Dorothy, My Gift from God.
Our love stronger than yesterday, weaker than tomorrow.

I wish to acknowledge the aid of Sean Wilson
who edited the manuscript but also did the cover.
Also, Dori Wilson and John Tomanelli
who worked so hard in making sure the book was published.

"Awake, arise, or be for ever fallen!"
Satan to his legions in hell after losing the battle for heaven,
from Milton's, Paradise Lost.

⇛ Prologue
Long Island, 1928

Lew Thomas fled through the woods and from the grounds of the hospital as he heard the wail of police sirens behind him. He dashed into the outskirts of the small village of Queens Park and past the startled onlookers on the porch of the town's only hotel, seeking desperately for a place to hide.

The voice of Belial, the fallen God, urged him onward. Belial filled his mind since he began to speak to him a week ago while Lew was undergoing treatment as a patient at the mental hospital. The voice frightened him and when he told one of the doctors of his experience, he increased Lew's drug dosage.

This morning, on Belial's command, Lew sacrificed three young female patients. When workers on the early shift arrived, they were horrified to find him forming the bodies in the shape of an inverted cross in the grassy circle in front of the Citadel.

As Lew turned into Main street, he heard the bells of the noon train to the city. He sobbed, straining for breath as he leaped onto the end of the train platform as the black model T Fords, with Police sirens screaming, raced into the station's graveled parking lot.

He frantically looked for an escape route as the locomotive thundered into the station. There were none as blue uniforms erupted from the cars and formed a ring around the station. Belial roared that Lew could easily vault the tracks, putting the incoming train between he and his pursuers. Lew leaped and had the sensation of floating as he cleared the rails.

Suddenly, Lew felt Belial leave his body and he gave a despairing wail just before the train smashed into him.

⇛ Chapter 1

The boy and girl, identical twins in looks, except for the pubescent breasts on the girl, shrank from the menacing figure of their mother as she herded them through the rear door of the farmhouse. A light evening breeze followed them as they cut down the hill and through the corn field of their farm. Their uncle silently joined them from his adjoining land as they crossed the state highway and entered Cold Spring Woods.

The coven was already assembled in a clearing not far from the spring that bubbled up with crystal clear water and gave the woods its name. A small fire danced in the center of the clearing and gave off just enough light to differentiate human shapes from the trees.

The coven was already dressed in black cloaks and hoods. The leader, outfitted in a red costume, the hood hiding his features, with only his goatee peering from under his cloak, held up his arms in supplication.

This was the children's first visit to the coven and they flinched as their mother roughly stripped the clothing from them. Their uncle leered appreciatively at the girl's slender figure as their mother pulled their capes and hoods from the burlap sack she carried.

Dressed, they joined their mother and uncle in the circle that formed around the fire. A vase, with goat's horns as handles was passed around the group. When it reached the children, they aped the others by grasping the vase by the goat's horns and drank deeply from the

1

vessel. The liquid was milky smooth and went down easily until it entered their stomaches. Then a fire seemed to explode through their bodies and the heat soared upward through their chest and into their brains.

The trees in the clearing began to rotate and the small fire in the clearing seemed to become a roaring inferno that sent fiery fingers reaching toward the sky.

A baby goat was held high by a hooded figure and another member held a vase under its throat. The hooded leader chanted verses and cut the kids throat, the blood pouring into the urn.

This vessel was also passed around the group. The dazed children were handed the vase and obediently brought the cup to their lips and drank from it. Several members of the coven began chanting and dancing around the fire. They heard the leader asking if they would be knights of Moloch. The children, in a psychedelic trance, chanted agreement.

The circle broke and cloaks were discarded and the nude figures coupled with each other, sometimes in groups of three. The girl was thrown to the ground and swiftly mounted by one of the men who ignored her cries of pain. It was their uncle.

The boy was taken by Tiny Barker, a migrant farm worker who had settled in the area after the last blueberry harvest. She was a huge woman, a mother of nine with pendulum like breasts hanging from her chest. Grinning and singing in a strange voice, she ran her tongue across his virginal erection. He ejaculated at once and she worked with hands and mouth to bring him to another hardness. This time she pulled him on top of her and guided him into her body.

Later he and the girl stood in a trance watching the couples sprawled around the fire, spent and motionless. The last couple to roll away from each other was their mother and uncle. The bearded figure was nowhere to be seen.

In a drugged daze, the children were led home by their silent mother. On the way, the boy attempted to hold his mother's hand. She angrily shook his hand away. It was the last time he attempted to seek any sign of affection from her. That night he began wetting his bed.

That night was only the first of many meetings with the coven. The memory of that first night and the last one, the terrible night the coven was destroyed haunted the twins for the rest of their short lives.

Later, when he finished high school with top honors, he was accepted into the medical program of N.Y.U on a scholarship and the nightmares continued. He worked at night as a bus boy at the Horn and Hardarts opposite Penn Station while living in a tenement apartment in Hells Kitchen. He began to experiment with the psychedelic drugs that were freely used by the college community.

He never forgot the lessons he learned in Cold Spring Woods when the cult, led by his mother sacrificed chickens and goats until that terrible night that the local farmers rose up and destroyed the coven of Satanic worshippers.

Drack was conceived that night in the Pines of New Jersey and fully formed in the dark streets of the West side of New York.

Cats and dogs were found slain and mutilated in the area under the West Side Highway. The slaughter continued until Drack accepted a position at the Queens Park Psychiatric Hospital on Long Island.

Kay Teehan awoke that morning feeling out of sorts and left with the remains of the headache she went to bed with the night before. She was secretly happy that Don didn't want sex when they went to bed. Kay thought it odd, since he was usually voracious in his sexual appetite when he came home from a road trip. She took some aspirin and felt well enough to go to her volunteer job at the nursing home.

Kay left Don in his office in the basement, filling out expense and business reports as was his habit on his first day home.

Her son, little Don, just turned sixteen, left for the private school he attended with a friend who picked him up in his car. She dropped her daughter off at her junior high school and started off to work. As Kay drove, her thoughts turned to Don and the recent lack of sex. She was surprised at the sudden warmth in her groin.

Smiling, she pulled into a rest stop on the expressway and on an impulse she called the nursing home from her cell phone and told them she wouldn't be in that day. Her attempts to reach Don were met with a constant busy signal. She thought that it was just as well, it would be a nice surprise for him.

Kay took the next exit and began to retrace her steps back home. As she drove, she became more aroused with each passing mile. The intensity surprised her since she never had the sexual fulfillment that she read about.

She was married at eighteen with a woeful lack of knowledge on sex. Her wedding night was a painful and messy experience. Don wanted sex long before she was ready and came almost as soon as he entered her. She did have one small orgasm when they had sex the first time after the birth of their son.

A second pregnancy resulted and when she began to swell, Don avoided her, going on long business trips, leaving her lonely and resentful. Kay had a long and painful birthing of their daughter and feared another pregnancy. She would submit to him on those rare occasions that he turned to her for sex. Her Catholic school education didn't have any classes or manuals on sexual relations. Her mother never discussed anything physical with her except to explain how to handle her monthly period. Kay's natural shyness prohibited her from discussing sex with her friends. When she heard other women describing their great orgasms, she attributed the stories to exaggeration.

Kay pulled into their driveway and was surprised to see their local oil distributor ringing their doorbell. She remembered that she had arranged an appointment for them to come to do their annual maintenance inspection and neglected to warn Don. Smiling to herself at the interruption of her plans, she and the oil man entered the house.

A blast of rock and roll assailed their ears as soon as she opened the door. Kay was amazed since Don normally demanded absolute quiet when he was doing his paperwork.

Kay led the oil man down the stairs to the basement and pointed out the room that contained their furnace. She noticed that the door to Don's office was closed and she opened it to tell him she was home and froze in shock. The young Danish nanny from next door was kneeling, mounted naked on top of Don on the couch. Her long brown hair was swaying gently as she ground her pelvic in a circular motion on him.

His eyes were bulging, staring at the girl whose own eyes were shut, lips pursed in determined concentration, tongue curled and slightly protruding.

As Kay screamed, they broke out of their trance and swung their heads towards Kay.

After the nanny scrambled into her clothes and fled past the gaping oil man, Don hastily dressed. Kay flew into an uncontrollable rage and ordered him out of the house.

It took her a week to come out of her shock long enough to contact a lawyer who immediately advised her to put a lock on their financial accounts. She acted too late. Don had cleaned out all the bank accounts and sold their stock portfolio. When her lawyer contacted his firm, Don had already resigned and cashed in his stock options. They claimed to have no idea as to his present whereabouts.

A few days later Kay received an anonymous call from a female who in a spiteful tone told Kay that Don had affairs on all his road trips and also with several women in the firm. The neighbor with whom the nanny lived told her that the girl disappeared at the same time as Don.

The household bills began coming in and Kay realized that she had to find a job and didn't have the faintest idea as to how to go about securing one. Her biggest worry was the lack of medical insurance. Within a month, she received a notice that the policy was cancelled upon Don's termination of employment. The notice did state that she could purchase the insurance but was appalled at the cost.

Her dilemma was compounded by the fact that her daughter was a diabetic and Kay knew that the treatments were terribly expensive.

As bills became overdue from the mortgage, joint credit cards, phone and other utilities, the dunning phone calls began. Her sister, who lived nearby was an immense help but ultimately, the only solution was to get a job.

She tried the ads in Newsday and found that she had little to offer in the way of formal job training. Her only qualification was some typing and shorthand courses she took while in high school. She never made use of these basic skills because she never held a job except as a housewife. The job market was tight at that time and company interviewers that she was able to see quickly lost interest.

She was a thirty six year old woman with no income and nothing to offer the business world.

Reluctantly, she settled for a job as a cashier in a local supermarket. The job paid minimum wages and barely covered her basic bills. She was able to maintain her utilities but could not do anything about paying the credit cards. Their dunning calls were the worst. She hated to answer the phone or pick up the messages from the answering machine.

Her sister's husband advised her to take computer courses at the local community college and offered to advance her the necessary tuition money.

Kay was hesitant about returning to school after being out of the educational scene for so many years. She accepted the loan and nervously signed up for business and computer courses at Suffolk Community College.

Kay excelled in all her courses by cramming every night and practicing on Don's computer after coming home from work.

A beneficial by-product occurred when she began taking notes in classes in shorthand. Some days she was putting in sixty hours including work, school and homework.

Kay began to grow in confidence and independence and found herself enjoying the sense of self worth from her excellent grades and the camaraderie of her much younger fellow students. Kay graduated from the two year school at the head of her class, carrying a 4.0 average.

One of her student counselors stated that she was eligible for a scholarship at Harvard. The Ivy league schools in particular were looking for female students in order to bolster their image. Kay was thrilled and toyed briefly with the idea but the dream was a short one. She had to get a well paying job with health benefits.

The only drawback to her new life was the children's reaction to Don's disappearance and her subsequent time away from home. At first they blamed the breakup on Kay and resented becoming latchkey kids and finding their allowance cut off. Her son was sullen and uncooperative around the house. He idolized his father, who took him on hunting trips and allowed him an occasional beer. Gradually, after not hearing from Don and being told the facts by the local gossips, her daughter, Eileen began to assist her by volunteering to do the household chores. Little Don was not as sullen but usually disappeared right after dinner. A busy Kay worried about him but her schedule left her too exhausted to do little about his attitude. Her daughter was able to secure a paper route and earn enough for the little things she wanted.

A friendly college guidance counselor gave her the lead she needed to finally make her independent. She advised her to get the Chieftain, a paper that specialized in listing all of the upcoming civil service tests in the state. She followed the counselor's advice and took as many as she could. It was one of these tests that landed her a position as a key punch specialist in the nearby Queens Park Mental Hospital. The pay was good but more importantly, the civil service had excellent insurance benefits.

The hospital was delighted to get her because of her college grades and more importantly, her shorthand ability. With the advent of hand held recorders, Gregg Shorthand became a lost art. She was immediately put to work taking dictation from doctors as they made their rounds in the wards or while interviewing patients and later transcribing the notes into the computer system.

⇒ Chapter 2

The cold October air whispered through the pines trees on the grounds of the institution. The sun hadn't quite disappeared in the west behind the buildings and its rays pointed long shadows toward the Long Island sound that formed one of the boundaries of the huge mental hospital.

The red brick buildings dotted the vast grounds of the sprawling state institution. The older buildings were located along the shore of the Long Island sound and the newer dwellings were perched on the boundary formed by the state highway. The new structures were depressingly similar in appearance unlike the buildings which were erected in the late 1890's.

The older buildings, with round towers at each of their corners, resembled the watchtowers of ancient European castles. The cornices were guarded by cement knights, huge swords held in both hands pointed at the skies. They stood at attention, staring vigilantly out to sea.

The highest structure was fourteen stories tall on a bluff facing the water. In 1910, the state cooperated with a Coast Guard request by placing powerful beacons in the two towers facing the sound. They were used as lighthouses until 1951 to aid shipping in the waters of the sound at night and in stormy weather. The building, nicknamed the

Citadel by the early residents was now condemned as unsafe and slated for demolition when one of the floors collapsed.

The building next to the Citadel housed the maintenance trucks and crews. Half of the structure was the home for the hospital police and fire department. It also served as the institution's power plant providing heat for the entire hospital. The building's oil fired generators served as back up for the institution when the power failed on the island as it often did during heavy storms. The huge phallic like smoke stack continually belched smoke from its furnaces.

One of the post-second world war patients, an elderly female holocaust victim, screamed in fear and went into traumatic shock upon seeing it for the first time after being admitted.

Mary Theresa O'Hara slipped through the tall pines and short scrub oak trees towards the water. Her blonde hair danced around her shoulders as a sudden breeze played with it and gently moved the fallen leaves over her toes and licked at her ankles. She held her jacket tightly around her trim figure against the evening chill. The only sign of life was a late flock of black necked Canadian geese wheeling into land in the pond, adjacent to the woods.

Her tiny fist clutched the wad of money that was to buy her freedom from the torment in her mind and the aching need in her body. She still couldn't believe her luck in being approached that afternoon with the offer to sell her the fix she so badly needed. It had been a shock when the doctor, of all people, offered it.

Mary smiled knowingly, remembering the sexual caresses the doctor gave her under the guise of a monthly physical. Perhaps she wouldn't have to use her money to get the drugs after all. Most of the younger female patients laughed as they recounted similar approaches from the doctor.

She paused briefly and looked upward as the roar of a low flying jet as it thundered overhead in its approach to La Guardia airport. Moving on, she licked her lips in anticipation and hurried faster as she spied a dim figure in white waiting for her in the shadow of two large pine trees. The doctor resembled one of the angels she had seen in the stained glass windows in the churches of her younger days in the Bronx, his long white gown flapping gently in the breeze coming from the waters of the sound.

The angel spread his hands wide as though in welcome, and smilingly she entered the embrace. Now she was positive that she wouldn't have to pay for the drugs after all. The angel was after sex like the rest of them. Her last conscious thought was that she had been hit on the side of her neck and didn't know that the knife had nearly decapitated her with it's first blow. As she fell, the angel threw himself upon the body and removed her clothing, one arm raising to the heavens and repeatedly slashing at the body.

Sergeant Jim Dane stood on the sidewalk in front of the precinct house waiting for his patrol car. The 86th Precinct, located in the heart of the Bronx, was in a state of flux. The precinct was responsible for a huge section of the borough with a mixed population of elderly people with the unmistakable pale skin and Celtic blue eyes of the Irish in startling contrast with the new immigrants with dark skin and hair. Each group passing the other as though they didn't exist. Dane thought, so much for the melting pot theory.

His driver edged his car out into the street from the parking lot which sided the precinct house. Dane slid into the passenger seat and nodded for the patrolman to proceed. He frowned as the unmistakable odor of alcohol drifted across the front seat.

They began their patrol by going north on 181st street and then into the teeming side streets, passing bodegas next door to Irish bars.

It was too early for the drug peddlers to be out in force but several young children raced into an old apartment house, obviously to warn someone of the approach of the patrol car. The drug sellers' popular distribution points were those houses with courtyards in front which provided egress to the many apartments. Thus, an early warning would allow a peddler to escape into one of many stairwells and into an apartment. Covered alleys linked some of the apartment houses similar to the catacombs of Rome. When a dealer was chased by the police, the alleys

These apartments were once considered the finest living quarters of the city with their great arches and internal mini parks. Built in the late 19th century, they became the homes for the rising middle class, mostly firemen, policemen and clerks for the office buildings of Manhattan. New York's magnificent subway system gave them swift access to their jobs in Manhattan. Wave after wave of immigrants gradually turned them into slums. When Jacob Riis built the great highway system and beautiful Parks on Long Island and Levitt built his low price homes, the veterans of World War 2 fled to the suburbs.

Dane told his driver to stop at a jewelry store on 181st Street on the way back from his tour. He had ordered a locket and the jeweler inscribed a message to his wife, Anna, for her birthday. Dane smiled in anticipation of her joyous laughter when she received any of his gifts, large or small.

Anna Dane drove into the parking lot of the Island Playhouse and sat for a moment, composing herself. She opened the rear door of the station wagon and let her two daughters out. Her heart tugged at their sheer beauty. Their features were that of Jim, fair of hair and pale skin. When they smiled, their faces had an aura of light and would attract answering smiles from people. Their figures, however, although of young children, were identical to hers, long legged and slender.

Smoothing the skirt over her leotard, she entered the theater. It was one of the most prestigious of the regional theaters that abounded in the Metropolitan New York area.

The Island Playhouse specialized in running revivals of Broadway musicals and its every play was reviewed by Newsday, and often by the Daily News. The plays were received unanimously as being close to being equal to the original Broadway run.

Anna attended several of the revivals at the playhouse as guests of friends in the cast. The playhouse was presently casting for a revival of the musical, Guys and Dolls. At her friends urging she went into the rigorous training that was needed to try out for the part of Adelaide in the musical. She was fortunate that one of her neighbors was a voice teacher and at Jim's urging, Anna began to take singing lessons again.

She waited nervously in the lobby as other actresses auditioned for the part of Adelaide. Her children played with one of her friends who was already selected for the role of Sarah, the lead. She smiled as she compared this audition to the ones she tried out for on Broadway before she met and married Jim Dane. Those auditions were held at the Actors Equity office in Manhattan and over five hundred girls usually showed up when openings were announced for a new play. Promptly at nine o'clock, their names were called and assigned a number. The doors were then shut and latecomers were turned away.

At one of the auditions, she won the role of understudy for the lead in an off Broadway show and occasionally played the part when the star was unable to perform. The director was impressed with her ability and wrote the necessary letter which helped get her card in Actor's Equity. Shortly thereafter she met Dane and became a policeman's wife and gave birth to two daughters in three years.

Dane was supportive of her desire to work in the local theaters. He understood the time she had to put into the dance classes and voice lessons before attempting her first audition.

Finally her name was called and she went into the theater and onto the stage. It was built along Elizabethan traditional lines wherein the stage was surrounded on three sides by tiers of seats. She noted that the lighting and sound were on par with many of the Broadway theaters.

The few people in the audience were reading her resume and obviously discussing her but stopped talking as she removed her raincoat. She was wearing a pink dressing gown through which a black, frilly, corset type leotard showed.

She had read in Back Stage, the bible for the theatrical profession, that actors auditioning for parts were no longer dressing in the theme of the play. Anna wanted the part of Adelaide so badly that she dressed for the part, leaving nothing to chance.

Anna chose "Adelaide's Lament" for her audition song from Guys and Dolls. She immediately dove into the character of the strong but fragile Broadway entertainer who loved the vacillating bookie, Nathan Detroit.

As soon as the piano player, a heavy set blonde woman began to play, Anna lost all nervousness and began her song, striding the stage, her gown trailing open, displaying her fine figure.

When she finished, those in the audience broke into unusual, enthusiastic applause. The director asked her to wait in the lobby, which was odd since she always had to wait for call backs for a part.

Anna drove her car up Seneca Road only two miles from home, mentally hugging herself with glee at the joy of landing the role of Adelaide. She glanced at the rear view mirror and smiled at her two daughters sitting in the rear seat, happy to be free of the boring and stressful audition.

When her attention swung back to the road, she was horrified to see a German Shepherd dog trotting across the highway in front of her. Instinctively, she swung the wheel to the right, avoiding the dog and the car climbed the slight incline at side of the road. She frantically spun the steering wheel to get the car back onto the highway.

She had time to scream once as the auto swerved back onto the road and crossed the center median straight into an oncoming gravel truck.

⇒ Chapter 3

Drack placed the two mounds of flesh and the triangle of skin and hair in the solution in the mason jar. They floated slightly below the surface and he leaned closer to examine his latest trophy. His hands were steady as he placed the lid on the container. It had only taken a few minutes to prepare the jar in the canning machine. He smiled remembering the hours his mother spent canning fruits, vegetables and the chickens he slaughtered. Placing the stupid chicken on the tree stump and bringing the ax down on its neck and watching it flopping was a thrill. He felt there was no more importance in taking the O'Hara girl's life than that of the chickens he killed. However, the sexual release and the slicing of his victim' breasts and vagina and adding them to his collection gave him eternal power over them. Viewing the body parts at his leisure brought back the sexual pleasure he felt when taking their lives.

He stepped back and admired the rest of his collection on the shelves. He had labeled the jars so that he could recall the name of the girl and the date that he took her. He recalled that the first one was not as exciting as he expected. No more so than the killing of any other animal. He did remember his surprise at the ease of covering his tracks. He leaned closer to the jar to read the name and *recalled the incident. She was a slut who rejected his advances and paid the price. The next ones became easier and more fulfilling.*

Jim Dane walked into the precinct house after his tour, carrying the gift locket for Anna. He sensed a difference in the sound of their voices as he passed the group of cops preparing for roll call. Some stopped talking and turned their heads away.

Tony Zaccheo, the granite faced administrator for the Precinct and Bill Kinnane waved at him to join them in Kinnane's office.

Dane, Tony and Kinnane had played on the Police Department baseball team as young men and remained friends through the years. The games between the Police, Fire and Sanitation Departments drew large crowds to the Polo Grounds up until the year they leveled the old stadium.

Kinnane, his leonine face set in solemn lines said, "Sit down Jim. You know Father Frank, our Chaplain and Ann Marino from our health unit."

"What the hell is going on?"

Kinnane looked down at his desk as he spoke, "Anna and the kids were in an accident on the road this afternoon."

The chaplain broke in, "Jim, I'm sorry, the children were killed instantly and your wife is in North Shore Hospital. We have a car waiting to take you there."

Dane looked wildly at the circle of men around him, unwilling to believe the horror he was hearing.

Kinnane stood, grasping Dane by the arm, "Come on Jim, we'd better get you to the hospital."

The tears started as he was led by the arms out through the silence of the office and down to the waiting patrol car. The driver started the siren and raced across the Throg's Neck Bridge and onto the Long Island Expressway.

Fortunately, traffic was light at this time of day and what little there was gave way for the wailing siren and flashing signal. The trip from the Bronx to the North Shore Hospital on Long Island was made in less than 20 minutes.

A nurse led them into Anna's room in the intensive care unit. Anna was laying face up, her eyes closed with two tubes hanging from what resembled a clothes tree dropping liquids into her arm. From the right side, a machine methodically hissed and hummed as it pumped oxygen into a tube extending from her mouth. A monitor at the top of the machine flashed their wavy lines across the screen and beeped in answer to her heartbeat.

Kinnane shook Jim from his trance, "I'll round up a doctor who can tell us what the score is."

Jim sat in a chair next to the bed and held one of Anna's hands. He spoke to her while massaging her hands, tears streaming down his face. Zaccheo stood at the foot of the bed moist eyed while the chaplain opened a prayer book and began reading silently.

Kinnane came back with a middle aged man in civilian clothes who led them to a small room across the hall. "I'm Doctor Abrams, a cardiologist who was here making calls when your wife was brought in. You really should be talking to the house doctor who was on duty when she was brought in."

"Why the tube into her mouth?"

"Her chest was crushed and a lung punctured. Her heart stopped beating on the table and we had to resuscitate her. They put a shunt into her throat and put her on the compensator to help her breathe." The man was clearly uncomfortable, "Look, you had better get hold of your family doctor and have him get all the information. You do have a family doctor?"

Jim nodded, "Doctor Orlando Santiago. He's taken care of the family since we moved to the island," then his voice, shaking, "where are my kids?"

The doctor said, "I really don't know any more than I've told you. We do have a Dr. Santiago on staff. I'll check and see if he's your man."

Kinnane took Jim firmly by the arm and led him back to Anna. "You stay here with Anna. I'll round up your doctor and bring him to the room. Father and Zaccheo will stay with you until I locate him."

Dane felt as though he was in a different time zone while the other world was crashing down and he was a spectator looking on. His mind was completely numb with the picture of a laughing Anna and happy children flooding his mind.

Dr. Santiago came in followed by Kinnane, the doctor's brown face grave and compassionate, "It's very bad Jim. She's not breathing on her own and her heartbeat is very erratic. Also, she has multiple fractures of her legs----"

The doctor stopped in mid-sentence at the look of pain on Dane's face as Dane had a mental picture of a smiling Anna as she danced in a costume from one of her musicals, "Will she make it? Is she going to live?"

Santiago hesitated, "She doesn't have much of a chance. It's only the machinery that's keeping her alive." The doctor was silent for a moment, "Have you and Anna ever discussed this type of eventuality?"

Dane nodded dully, "She was always emphatic that she didn't want to be kept alive like some medical freak. I felt the same way and we had a living will drawn up several years ago." Dane began weeping again, "Christ! I always thought that I would be the first to go."

"Do you want to take her off the compensator?"

Dane shook his head. "I can't. Not yet. Where are the children?"

"Downstairs." Meaning the morgue.

_____

The mass and burial of the two little white caskets were an emotional nightmare for Dane that was only interrupted by visits to the hospital.

Dr. Santiago prescribed sleeping pills that enabled Dane to get some rest. On the fifth morning after the accident, Dane was preparing to leave for the hospital, when the phone rang. "Jim, this is Dr. Santiago." the doctor then lapsed into silence.

Jim said dully, "She's gone?"

"She passed away five minutes ago."

"Tell them not to move her out of that room until I get there and tell them to take that damned tube out of her throat."

He realized that he had questions to ask her that she would never hear and how much he treasured her. Never.

After the funeral, Dane insisted on returning home alone to their home. He refused the offers of family and friends who suggested he move in with them, if only temporarily. He became a recluse, leaving the house only to buy liquor when his supply ran out. Kindly neighbors brought trays of food that he would heat in the microwave when he was hungry. Seeing pictures of Anna and the children would fire him into spasms of deep sobbing. The phone would ring incessantly until he took it off the hook. Alcohol became his narcotic.

He refused to answer the door and only opened it to let the cat in or out. He began to seriously contemplate suicide, knowing he wouldn't he wouldn't be the first cop to eat his gun. He remembered someone telling him that sometimes it was harder to live than to die.

One morning, there was an incessant pounding at the door and the voice of Kinnane bellowing, "Jim, if you don't open the door, we're going to break in."

When Dane heard the first thud against the door, he opened it a crack and saw Kinnane and Zaccheo with several friends from the force, "I don't want you here. I don't need you here. Go away."

When Jim tried to close the door, the men shouldered their way through. They went to work immediately cleaning up the house, forcing him to make decisions regarding Anna and the children's clothes. They went through every drawer in the house putting Anna's jewelry into a bag and collecting all his uncashed paychecks and had him endorse them. Kinnane had him sign the insurance papers and the authorization for a lawyer to handle the accident case. He then went through his mail and wrote checks to bring his bills up to date.

Finally, when everything was in order and the house was neat and clean, the men left with the exception of Kinnane, "I'm staying here with you through the night and the men have agreed to babysit you until you're ready to come back to work."

"Fuck you and the job."

Kinnane sighed, "We're covering you on roll call every day, so that you don't miss time. We're not kidding anyone downtown but there is only so much they'll take. You have to start coming in if only to show your face. You have five years to go before putting in your papers. Don't waste all the time you've put into the job."

They took turns staying with him day and night, controlling his drinking and making sure he ate on a regular basis.

Dane finally drove in with Kinnane and was assigned to an eight to four shift. He carried a hip flask and drank from it in order to survive the times when memories would flood back. It became his habit after his tour to stop at The Shield, a bar, that was a cops hangout, two blocks from the precinct. Most of the men in the bar avoided him. A few of the old timers would nod and say hello. He began to get a reputation for turbulent behavior.

He was up twice on charges of using unnecessary force on minority citizens. The successful defense was that Fort Apache was comprised of ninety percent minority citizens. The department psychiatrist labeled him as violence prone and recommended he be transferred to a desk job.

It was a standing joke in the station house by his fellow policemen that he wasn't racist, he was violent with everybody.

A few times he was pulled over on the expressway for drunken driving. He was always let go when they saw his shield. Finally, so many complaints were received by his commander from the Nassau police that he was ordered to stop driving to work. Dane began taking the Long Island Railroad to work and was delighted to find that he could now drink all the way home by riding in the club car. The early morning trains didn't have a bar car but he learned from a fellow tippler to buy a Big Slurpee from the Seven Eleven near the station. The trick was to spill half of the drink out and replace it with Vodka. Thus, he was able to sip alcohol on the long commute to work. His life became a scripted play as he slipped into the world of the functioning alcoholic.

One day, while on routine patrol, a call went over the police radio for backup for a domestic dispute in the block they were on. Dane normally ignored these calls but his driver insisted they answer the call since they were right at the scene. They stopped and the driver immediately got out and raced up the stairs. Dane in an alcoholic daze, slowly and reluctantly entered the house. It was one of the fine old Bronx apartment buildings that had gone to seed. The halls reeked with the sweet odor of marijuana and the pungent smell of urine.

He followed the sounds of conflict to the third floor and found his driver and two uniforms battling a huge negro woman wielding an iron skillet. As he went to draw his revolver, she broke free and charged Dane, hitting him with the skillet, knocking him head over heels down the stairs. Semi-conscious, he catapulted down until his leg caught between two of the banister supports. As he tumbled down the stairs, he heard the unmistakable boom of a shotgun. He mercifully passed out as his leg snapped with a terrible noise.

He woke up in the hospital to see a nurse leaning over him and felt the fire of pain that ran down his right leg. "Good morning Mr. Dane."

"Where am I?"

"You're in the Cornell Medical center orthopedic ward. You've been pretty much out of it for the past two days."

"Two days?"

She nodded, "I wasn't on duty when they admitted you but your chart at the nurses station says you had a severe concussion when they brought you in."

"What the hell is wrong with my leg?"

"Dr. Schneider, our orthopedic specialist is in the ward right now. He should be in to see you and tell you about your problems."

Dane's nerves were screaming from the pain and the need for a drink. Mercifully, the nurse gave him a pill that calmed his nerves.

A short time later the doctor came in to see him. Dane went right to the point, "What the hell is wrong with my leg?"

The man frowned, "You were thrown down a flight of stairs. Apparently you caught your leg between the legs of the banister and snapped it. The banister broke and you continued falling, breaking it in several more places."

Dane vaguely recalled mounting the stairs and seeing the black woman fighting with the other cops, "I remember hearing a shotgun going off. Was I shot in the leg.?"

The doctor grimaced, "No. An officer following you up the stairs saw you and thought you were dead. When he saw the woman advancing on the other officers he shot her. It made all the papers."

"How soon will I be able to walk?"

"We set the bones that we were able to work on but I am going to have to operate on the femur that was shattered. We couldn't do that until you came out of the concussion. I'm going to have to put a pin in your leg to give the leg some support."

The break and subsequent operation left him with one leg slightly shorter than the other and made him unfit for active duty. In the weeks that followed his release from the medical center, Dane exercised in a rehab program at a hospital near his home.

He joined a local YMCA and used the exercise equipment and swam in its pool incessantly. He purchased a treadmill and weight equipment and worked out every night until he fell into bed completely exhausted. His body was fit and trim as that of a twenty year old but didn't change the fact that his right leg was an inch shorter than his left.

There was a huge and unexpected benefit. His fierce attempt at healing his leg drove the need for daily drinking from his system. Dane awoke one morning and threw all the liquor bottles in his house into the garbage.

He was offered a three quarter disability pension or an opportunity to work on desk duty in the records department until his twenty years were completed. The insurance case was settled and the money put into the hands of a stock broker friend for investment. The money was repugnant to Dane and his police pay was more than enough for his needs.

Dane hated the paper work and one day two years later, when he was having lunch with Zaccheo, "Jim, I have something that might be of interest to you." He passed a police bulletin over the table to him, "We get notices from time to time from cities and counties across the nation who are looking for cops from New York City to head their departments. We have a nationwide reputation for excellent training. You remember your old precinct Captain from the 78th? When he retired he immediately got a plush job heading up a law enforcement department in Orange County, California."

"Yeah. Jimmy Trainor. He asked me a couple of times to go out there to join him when I put in my papers. I've turned him down because I can't leave Anna and the kids."

"This isn't from him. It's about an opening in a mental hospital in Suffolk County for someone to head up their police force. It's right in your back yard." He looked obliquely at Dane, "And another five minutes from their graves."

"Christ, that's a rent-a-cop job."

"No, it's not. The place is like a small city. They have seventeen men on the force. They have five patrol cars and their own building. It has great perks. You get a company car, state medical benefits and the pay is almost what you're making here."

Dane hesitated, then shook his head, "I like the city. I know it's a pain in the ass commuting, but I've only got a couple of years to go and then maybe I'll take Trainor up on his offer."

Zaccheo handed him the bulletin, "Do me a favor. At least go out and talk to them. You hate that job you're in now. This will give you a chance to do what you do best, train cops."

Dane made an appointment with the hospital administrator and drove out to the institution. The drive was only ten minutes, door to door from his home to the main entrance of the hospital.

It was bright and sunny the day of his interview and when he arrived at the hospital, he paused to admire the view of the grounds. From the main gate, the land sloped gradually down to the Long Island Sound. The green of the lawns was a spectacular contrast to the blue green waters of the sound and the air that day was so clear that the Connecticut shore seemed to be within touch.

The beauty of the scenery made the drab buildings that dotted the landscape ugly and foreboding.

He was impressed with the committee that interviewed him and the opportunity to be out on the street again. The hospital and state people were delighted with his background and after three meetings offered him the job.

The graves of Donna and his daughters were between the hospital and home. He turned off at the road leading to the cemetery and parked on a curve leading to the graves. He stood over the graves, sobs racking his body. Somehow he felt sure that Anna wanted him out of the city.

On the way home from the cemetery, he passed a local liquor store and on impulse, he stopped and bought a bottle of wine. He drank two glasses with dinner and didn't feel the driving need to continue drinking. The move was right for him.

He took the three quarters disability retirement plan from the force and reported two weeks later as Captain of the Queens Park Mental Hospital security force.

⇒ Chapter 4

Drack left the Teehan woman's office and locked the door behind him. He hadn't found anything incriminating that he could report to the authorities. The slut had nothing on her desk but pictures of her brats and three patient files. The files shouldn't have been left on her desk over the weekend, but it was not enough violation of hospital policy to cause her a problem. He had begun to seek evidence to get her censured when she rebuffed his advances. It was his habit on a weekend to visit the staff offices on weekends when the hospital was empty of personnel. When he found something that was awry he would make an anonymous phone call the following Monday to the person's supervisor.

He carefully examined the parking lot to be certain that he would not be observed leaving the admissions building. It was a bright, crisp fall day and the afternoon sun was warm enough that he wore only his long, white hospital gown over his suit.

Walking to his car, his attention was diverted to crowd noises emanating from the adjacent area where the sport complex was housed. The complex was actually a baseball diamond and soccer field that was put up originally for the hospital teams to play.

At one time, the hospital baseball team was good enough to challenge the semi professional teams from all over the Island. Covered stands were built to accommodate the huge amounts of people that came to watch the games.

The hospital soccer team was started by the waves of Irish immigrants who flooded the area to go to work for the hospital. The teams were disbanded and the fields were left to ruin when television began broadcasting games from Ebbet's field and Yankee Stadium. The complex was now used only on the weekends by the CYO and PAL teams of Queens Park.

Walking to the top of the hill overlooking the field, Drack saw that a girl's soccer match was in progress. The center forward of the visiting team had just broken through Queens Park defenses and scored a goal. Drack became aroused as he watched the teenage girls, their breasts bouncing under their gaily covered uniform shirts as they ran the field.

Suddenly, one of the spectators came out from the stands and began walking up the hill towards him. He stepped behind the tree when he recognized the girl as being one of his patients, Peggy Wainwright. He began to walk in a direction that was sure to intercept her.

Red O'Dwyer and Tommy Izzo had just finished selling their supply of drugs to their customers in the stands and to the high school students that lined the soccer field.

Red spotted the Wainwright girl walk to the top of the hill of the complex and disappear from sight. Turning to Tommy he asked, "You got any crack left?"

"Yeah."

"I just say Peggy W. head up the hill. She's one great piece of ass. She'll do anything for a hit."

Grabbing the sandwich bag of coke, Red ran to the top of the hill in time to see the Wainwright girl talking to a doctor on the path. He said "Shit!" and sat down.

The doctor suddenly reached for the girl's breasts and she whirled and twisted free of his embrace. Running halfway down the hill to the coffee shop, she turned and with a taunting laugh, gave him the finger. The doctor stood staring after her until she disappeared into the coffee shop. He turned and strode angrily up the hill.

Red grinned and sat down to wait.

⇒ Chapter 5

Drack sat in his collection room savoring the jars of trophies that he accumulated over the past eight years. His head ached with fury at the memory of the Wainwright slut rejecting him and the voices started. They told him to kill came more frequently now. In the beginning he was able to control the voices so that he could perform his duties at the hospital and he was able to be careful in his selection of victims that were not going to be missed. Lately, the voices were more strident and ordering him to be reckless in his actions.

The sluts were always big breasted young girls with a history of drug abuse and usually were the ones who rebuffed his advances. He became calmer as he fondled the jars containing the trophies, remembering. The memory of their terror and their screams of pain would arouse him and he would masturbate until the tension was released.

His two biggest problems were the taking of the victims on the busy grounds of the hospital and the disposal of the remains. When the opportunity presented itself, he preferred to bring the victims to his home and kill them there.

He once tried to dispose of one body by putting it in the huge furnace that supplied heat to the institution. A passing hospital security patrol almost discovered him bringing the remains into the building. From then on he buried his victims at night in a little used section of the hospital grounds.

The new police chief of the security force worried him. He was unlike the previous chief who cared about nothing but his alcohol and preying on the sexual appetites of the young female patients. The new man had the look of a hunter and was stepping up night patrols on the grounds. Besides, he was obviously taken with the Teehan woman, who for many reasons, strangely excited Drack.

Kay Teehan looked up as Donna Burns walked into her office and stopped typing the latest admittance to the hospital into the computer. She stretched her arms in an effort to relieve the tension from the long hours on the keyboard, and removed her glasses, rubbing her eyes.

Kay's slacks were bunched up on her full figure and she looked enviously at Donna's slender frame outlined in her form fitting nurse's dress. Donna was one of the few nurses that still favored a dress instead of the white slacks that the younger women wore to work. She confessed to Kay that she knew that the white dress showed off her fine legs and figure better than slacks. Donna kept her shoulder length blonde hair in the same tinted shade and style as Kay. The coloring of gold and white made her a striking figure against the drab hospital background.

Ruefully, she admitted that it did her little good since most of the doctors and pyschs in the hospital were either puritanical Orientals or Indians and all were married. She felt that the few, unattached white doctors were too young for her, although she flirted outrageously with them and acknowledged to Kay of affairs with two of the doctors still on staff.

Kay was shocked at first by Donna's frankness in her admission to frequenting the singles bar in the area for "action to satisfy her needs".

They became close friends and lunched together in the hospital cafeteria almost every day but Kay refused the offer to join her at night in the singles scene.

Kay quickly learned that Donna was a kind and loyal friend who counseled and guided her through the first few months at work at the hospital. The pretty woman, like Kay, married very young and also bore two children and, like Kay, a boy and a girl. Her husband, a fireman died of a heart attack while battling a blaze in the city. The insurance and pension left her financially independent but when her son joined the fire department and her daughter married, Donna went back to nursing in order to keep busy.

Kay found it overwhelming to start a career after the years raising children and running a home. After her husband's desertion, she found it frightening to be without funds and having to be the decision maker for the family.

Donna's earthiness and good humor turned the uncertainty and loneliness of those first few months into laughter and enjoyment.

Donna smiled at Kay and picked up one of the completed forms from the out box., "You keep admitting them and they keep walking off happy valley. We should install a revolving door at the main entrance."

Kay laughed and looked up. "Who jumped the fence now?"

Donna laughed. "What fence? The only fence on the grounds is the Berlin Wall we have around "Murderer's Row.""

Kay shuddered, Murderers Row was the only building that truly frightened her. It housed the most vicious and depraved of the homicidal maniacs that were being sent to Queens Park as the state closed other institutions. The fence that Donna was referring to was actually a barricade composed of two fences with the inside one made of reinforced wire with razor sharp barbed spikes hanging over the top. The second fence was a massive brick wall thirty feet high and constructed six feet behind the wire fence and also topped with rolls of barbed wire. The barricade was erected when a violent patient scaled a simple wire fence and was caught while attacking a woman in one of the nearby homes.

In order to avoid the building and the fence, Kay drove on to the grounds through an entrance from the state highway which took her out of her way when coming to work.

Kay flinched as Donna said, "The O'Hara kid skipped out last night."

"I don't believe it!"

Donna nodded. "She had a pass to go to the coffee shop after dinner and wasn't missed until bedtime. The police checked the town and the late trains. She wasn't on any of them." She shrugged. "She must have hitched a ride."

Kay was depressed at the news, "Poor kid. I really liked her and thought she was gonna make it." Kay shook her head. "When she was admitted, she was in such bad shape. The booze and drugs had her on another planet."

"You keep getting too close to some of these patients and you'll wind up with a problem. It's happened before. A few years ago one of our social workers fell for one of her charges. When he signed himself out, she had him move in with her. He wound up killing her and her two kids."

Kay pursed her lips, "The O'Hara girl wasn't violent. She was a sweet kid, with so much going for her."

Donna looked out the tiny window at the circle where a police wagon had just arrived followed by a patrol car. A huge blonde young man with manacles on wrists and ankles was helped out of the back of the wagon and meekly turned around so that one of the officers could unlock the ankle restraints.

As soon as he was released, he kicked the first officer in the groin and swung a vicious two handed blow to the head of the second. The patrol car erupted and two troopers sprang out to help the men. Two aides raced out from the building and joined the melee.

Donna gasped. "Oh my God, we've got another violent one and he's a giant." She pushed a button and a klaxon horn blared as she grabbed the mike for the intercom and repeated, "Code three. Code three. Code three in front of admissions." She dropped the mike and raced outside, knowing that all the medical personnel in the building would answer a code three alert.

More aides appeared to join the battle. The patient seemed to have superhuman strength as he easily threw the men around him like so many toys.

Kay arose and watched as the battle swayed in a swirl of white clad aides and blue uniforms attempting to bring the man down. A hospital patrol car pulled up and two more men joined the fray. Kay's heart jumped as she recognized one of the men as Jim Dane, the new head of the hospital's small police force.

Incredibly, the patient broke free twice and began to run until tackled by a burly aide. Two of the county cops were down, one lying still, the other on hands and knees, looking at the ground as though searching for something he lost. One of the county cops, a red headed sergeant, ran to his squad car and came racing back with a club. The officer, a man of stocky build, graying at the temples and with a florid complexion, flaming with exertion, swung the truncheon at the patient's head. The man ignored the first two lows although his struggle began to lessen. The third blow brought the patient to his knees, still struggling. Donna appeared with a straight jacket and the man was finally subdued and dragged bleeding into the lobby. One of the aids, a husky brutish man had an angry welt on the side of his face where the athlete had struck him. He glared down malevolently at the at the athlete, obviously hoping for more resistance from the man so as to further punish him.

A few minutes later Donna appeared back in the office with Jim Dane and the sergeant in tow, talking animatedly as they entered the room. "That was fun. I've been a nurse here for twenty-one years and in the beginning, I could handle just about every patient on the grounds by myself." She shook her head, "They keep getting bigger and more violent each month."

The sergeant smiling, handed a folder to Kay. "Mrs. Burns says that you were to get the papers on that package we delivered."

Donna smoothed her hair, knowing the cop was smiling at her as she spoke, "What in the world was Hercules on?"

"We found angel dust on him when we picked him up last night, tearing a bar apart in Southport. He went bonkers in night court and the judge felt he better come here for evaluation." The sergeant grinned, "He's a pro football player in town for a game with the Jets. It looks like he's gonna miss the game."

Kay spoke as she entered the data into the computer on the man. "He's the tenth really bad one we've taken in this month including a cannibal and a minister who thinks he's god. What in the world will we get next?"

The sergeant laughed, "A minister who thinks he's God doesn't sound so bad."

Kay looked up. "He killed his wife and three children upstate. He said Abraham spoke to him and promised that they would rise from the dead in three days."

"Jesus, how can you women stand working here?"

"I'm the sole support of two kids and Donna is a widow who swears she's going to retire at least once a month." Kay smiled at Dane. "Most of the women working here are in the same boat.

Donna broke in. "When I first came here as a young nurse, most of our patients were docile and easy to control. Quite a few were elderly people who signed themselves in because they had no place else to go. It's only in the past few years that we started getting the druggies and killers."

Kay handed the sergeant a receipt for the patient, "I've only been here two years and in that short a time I've seen the change in the hospital's population. Originally, most of them were senile people or the retarded who were dumped here by their families."

Donna nodded, "When we started getting the criminally insane here and some of the retarded children were sexually abused, even the politicians realized that the kids had to be moved."

The sergeant shook his head and eyed Dane curiously. "I'm Pat Nugent. You're new here aren't you?" He measured Dane. "You an ex-cop? You handled yourself like one out there."

Dane nodded. "Good guess. I was on the job in the City."

"You look too young to have pulled the pin."

"I'd still be there except for an accident. I worked out of Fort Apache and was on the street when we got a call that there was a domestic disturbance in the next block. My driver and I took the call and when we walked in on the scene, there were two cops getting beat up by a woman on the third floor. When I stepped in to help, she threw me down a flight of stairs, breaking my leg in three places."

"Four cops and you couldn't handle one woman."

Dane stared impassively at the sergeant for a moment, with cold blue eyes. "She weighed over three hundred pounds, and was skulled on crack. She was damn near as strong as our boy out there." Dane took a deep breath, "Anyway to answer your question, when the breaks healed, they left me with one leg shorter than the other. I was offered the choice of three quarter disability or a desk job in records. I did that for awhile and when a friend of mine told me this place was looking for someone," He shrugged. "I hated the desk work and liked this area so I took the job."

Nugent, respect in his voice, shook hands. "I'll be seeing you again. Lately, half of our calls in this part of the precinct are here at the hospital." With that he turned to leave, "Can someone tell me where to find a Doctor Younger? Our pistol license division spoke to him about a month ago. He has a patient in here who has a license to carry a gun. We asked him for a letter regarding the guy so that we can void his permit. We never got an answer and they asked me to pick up a letter on my next trip in here."

Donna grabbed the sergeant by the arm and said hastily over her shoulder. "I'll take him to Younger. I'll see you guys later."

Kay heard the cop asking Donna how her husband had died as they left the office together. She leaned her head in her hands wondering where the O'Hara girl had gone. It seemed as though a young girl was skipping out at least once a week.

Dane said sympathetically. "Don't let it get to you."

"It's just that this week has been so tense. We have an inspection team in from Albany for certification on Monday. If we don't pass, we lose some of the state funding, so everyone goes a little crazy around here." She shook her head, "and now the O'Hara girl skipped out. I really liked her."

"I know I'm a new guy in town, but isn't there an awful lot of young girls walking out of here?"

She gave him a troubled smile. "When I bring up the subject of all the girls escaping, everybody laughs at me. Apparently, there's always been a problem keeping the young ones here."

Dane shook his head. "It's no wonder with all the areas that are wide open." He changed the subject, saying, "I'll see you outside on the steps in front by four-thirty tonight and we'll grab a bite to eat at the Old Pier before going to the play. that way we can get to the park early enough to get decent seats."

She nodded shyly, "I love Shakespeare in the park and Romeo and Juliet. Hamlet has always been a favorite of mine."

"I prefer Hamlet, but I'm looking forward to tonight."

She nodded her head but lost her smile as a tall, square, gray haired woman with granite like features entered the office with forms in her hand. With her was a heavy set man dressed in a suit, his jacket open and his belly bulging against his shirt. Without preamble, he demanded, "Mrs. Teehan, make a copy for me of the file on that patient that was just admitted."

When Kay hesitated, the doctor who was with the man said, "It's alright Mrs. Teehan. This is Mr. Gunn, one of the patients' legal advocates. He is responsible for this wing and will be handling this patient's case."

Kay left the room with the file to make a photo copy for the lawyer. As she left, Gunn turned to Dane, "Weren't you one of the men that was involved in getting that football player under control?"

Dane nodded.

"I hope you weren't one of the men who clubbed him into submission. When he is coherent, I'm going to see if he wants to sue."

Dane was angered at Gunn's pompous tone, "The bastard was throwing people around like rag dolls. No, I didn't hit him, but if I had I had a club handy I would have used it. That son of a bitch was trying to kill people." With that he stormed out of the room passing a startled Kay telling her he would be waiting for her in the circle outside of admissions.

⇒ Chapter 6

Drack entered his house and turned on the floodlights illuminating the grounds. He carefully locked the front door and breathed a sigh of relief. The house was his womb of safety and the voices of Belial and Lew were silent.

The house was built in the early 1900s and designed in the Colonial style as were all the homes on doctors row at the hospital. It was really too big for one person and the two story wooden buildings were hot in the summer and expensive to heat in the winter. Since the hospital paid for the utilities, the house was one of the perks that was used to recruit doctors.

Each home was located on a full acre of land, insuring privacy for its occupants. The grounds were once well manicured by a large staff of gardeners but they were the first to be released when the state began cutting the budget for mental health. Lately, the trees and shrubbery became overgrown through lack of attention. The lawns surrounding the homes became wild and matted except for the few tenants who cared enough to mow.

The maintenance people were supposed to paint the houses every other year but the latest cutbacks left the hospital without enough manpower to keep up to the schedule. The paint began to peel and crack, giving the homes a seedy look. Some of the Doctors began to bring patients home to do the maintenance work under the guise of it being therapeutic.

His neighbors on either side were Orientals who kept to themselves. They, nor anyone were ever invited into his home and Drack declined all social invitations. People who occasionally came to the door seeking donations or the like were harshly rebuffed and nobody had bothered him at home for years.

Through the years, he painstakingly redecorated each room in a different motif and covered the windows with heavy drapes. One of his favorite rooms was on the second floor that he painted a brilliant red and filled with heavy, dark Spanish furniture. The walls were covered with paintings depicting Dante's Inferno that he picked up from the small art galleries around Greenwich Village. The centerpiece of the room was a huge, violent oil painting, entitled *The Screaming Head*. He found it one Sunday while strolling Fifth Avenue, viewing the artists open air exhibition, their paintings leaning against the cobblestone wall that serves as a boundary for Central Park. He was attracted to the painting because the artist was an attractive young girl who flirted with him until he paid for the painting.

The other rooms were painted in light colors, most with a brilliant white, some furnished with but a single chair in the center.

The exception was the basement. The walls were bare save for the metal shelves lined with mason jars and a huge cold storage locker in the corner. Cone shaped and triangular pieces of flesh were floating in fluid in the jars.

He called it his collection room and was happiest here.

One of the sidewalls contained a huge wooden door. When Drack first took possession of the house he discovered the catacombs that ran under the older buildings were adjacent to his basement *and he broke through the wall leading to the tunnels. He constructed a door in the wall and camouflaged it on the tunnel side so that he had hidden access to the catacombs.*

Years ago, the hospital grounds were used primarily as a farm that supplied the food to patients and staff and the surplus sold to the townspeople. During the winter, products of the farm such as potatoes, yams and apples were stored in the dark, cool cellars of the buildings.

Gradually, as new buildings were added, an underground labyrinth was dug from root cellar to root cellar to connect the buildings to enable the staff to travel between buildings in inclement weather. As the automobile grew in popularity and used by the staff to travel between buildings, the underground passageways fell into disuse. The only surface indications that they existed were short, round pillboxes with square holes in their sides. They dotted the land where air shafts were dug to keep the air clean and filter out the fumes from the kerosene and oil lamps that were used to light the passageways.

Most of the people who worked at the hospital were unaware of their existence. Drack found out about them from one of his patients who worked part time in a grocery store in the village. The patient heard about the tunnels from the owner of the store who worked at the hospital until his retirement.

The few old timers left on the hospital staff and knew of the passageways never entered into the tunnels because of the dampness and lack of light.

Drack became curious and explored all the tunnels in his spare time and felt a power in the knowledge that he was able to move from building to building without being seen. Through the years he roamed the tunnels every night and reveled in his secret and the comfort the womb like feeling they gave him.

As he grew familiar with the layout of the catacombs and their entrances into the buildings, he drilled peepholes through the walls of the tunnels into the buildings. This enabled him to inspect a building before entering and possibly being surprised by someone in the basement. The hospital staff used many of the basements to store old files and occasionally there was a female patient in the basement either storing files or researching an old one. The hospital occasionally used a patient to do simple clerical work.

The psychiatrists felt that this was an excellent form of therapy. Drack would take one of these when they were young, female and the right opportunity presented itself. They were the best victims since it was a simple matter of dragging them through the tunnels to his collection room. There he would work on them at his leisure. Their screams brought him to his highest level of pleasure.

The hospital staff always assumed that the patient had slipped from the grounds.

The caverns were lit by torches or lanterns that were lit and placed in special holders. The authorities started to electrify the tunnels, but one of the many austerity programs halted the construction and the project was never completed.

That night was a disaster. As soon as he entered Building 22, a nurse rushed out to him with the news that a patient called Popeye had somehow obtained a bottle of whiskey, and after drinking it, became suicidal.

Popeye was normally a quiet, cheerful man, who adopted the persona of the comic book character, to the point of wearing a sailor costume, including an old yachting cap and demanding spinach with every meal.

Drack was brutal in his treatment of the man and ordered two aids to bind him in a restraining sheet. The night duty nurse was obviously shocked and disapproved of the treatment of the well liked Popeye.

He finished his hospital rounds, tired and angry and started his car, anxious to get home. The schedule called for him to be on call all night.

He was still disturbed at seeing that nice Teehan woman at the Old Pier with the new police chief when he went in there, earlier for dinner. As he was leaving, she stopped him and introduced him to Dane. He felt she was mocking him by showing off her latest conquest. As was his wont, he stopped and peered through the big picture window of the restaurant when he left after finishing his meal. The woman was sitting with Dane at a table directly in front of the window. They were talking animatedly and occasionally touching each other's hand.

As he drove away from the restaurant anger filled him and he gripped the steering wheel tightly as he pictured the cops dirty hands running over her firm, full breasts. A familiar scene flashed into his mind of his mother bare to the waist and the hands groping her. He held his head as the whispers began. Drack frantically reached into the pocket of his jacket and pulled out a cigarette case. He snapped it open and picked out of the array of pills, two Prozac capsules and swallowed them. The drugs had an immediate effect, momentarily blurring his vision but giving him a sudden surge of power.

As he pulled out of the parking circle, and headed up the shortcut to the main boulevard, he jumped as Lew Thomas spoke to him. Lew and Belial rarely appeared to him at the same time but

43

now he heard Belial whispering in the background as Lew spoke, "It's time to punish that little whore, the Wainwright girl."

As Lew finished speaking, the Wainwright girl was coming into view, walking from the workshop area, hurrying to get to her ward before curfew. The last rays of the late sun were peering over the trees that lined the road. Drack shook his head, fearfully. "I'm not ready. It's too bright, I'm sure to be seen."

Belial's red, grinning, bearded face appeared on the windshield, "Moloch, king of human sacrifice demands you obey! When you stood in the circle with the rest chanting our names and calling us out of eternity, you vowed to be faithful. When you partook of the human sacrifice you swore an oath to obey us forever."

Drack whimpered, "I was young_____."

Belial's roar was that of gigantic waves crashing upon his ears. "When we were cast down from heaven, we called our legions from the burning lake, knowing we couldn't regain the heavily guarded ramparts of heaven and decided to conquer this pit." He sneered, "You promised that you were going to be one of our knights to help in the conquest."

Suddenly, his voice became lower and silky "But, have no fear, we are with you and you won't need the knife this time. For now, just stop her breathing. Put her in the trunk of the car and we can bring her to our collection room."

Drack covered his ears with his hands in a vain effort to shut out the bellowing voice of Belial. He was unable to refuse them ever since they first came to him that day in the treatment library.

He had accidentally picked up and read Lew's case history and of his sudden violence and suicide in the train station. The first whispers started then along with the resurrection of the buried memories of his childhood. Their power over him became stronger after every sacrifice.

They taught him to be careful in his actions while working and to use his knowledge of psychiatric drugs to keep him functioning normally in his daily routine. Belial and Thomas completely ruled him. There was nobody to hear the strange voices coming to him.

The voices faded as the thought of the Wainwright girl in his collection room brought fire to his groin. She would pay for her laughter at the soccer field. With his mind and body aflame, he slowly brought the car to a halt. The girl recognizing him, hesitated for a moment, then shrugging accepted his offer of a lift to her dorm. Her red hair was tousled by the wind and she turned to him with a coquettish smile that reminded him of his mother when she was drinking and with a man.

Her smile threw him into a violent rage and he threw a tremendous back hand to the girls face. Her head snapped back and then forward as he suddenly applied the brakes. He reached across her semiconscious body and opened the door and pushed her halfway out. He glanced quickly around. The area looked completely deserted.

Drack ran around the car and dragged the girl to the back of the car. As he opened the trunk, she moaned, he stripped her of jacket and blouse and savagely ripped her bra from her. He paused momentarily, as her full breasts fell free of the garment. He moaned and turned the girl over and swiftly tied the bra around her throat and with hands on either side of the bra leaned back, straining with the exertion of the execution. His body trembled with spasms of repeated orgasms in response to her death throes. Belial was screaming what a fool he was to have killed her instead of taking her to his collection room.

As he arose, a sound caused him to whirl around and he gasped as he saw a figure standing rigidly next to a tree at the side of the road. He froze as he watched the man turn and walk calmly towards the main boulevard. With sudden relief, he recognized the figure. It was the catatonic professor who would only answer to a direct question and then in one syllable words.

Dane sat in his office initialing the time sheets for the week, impatient for the clock on the wall to move faster to the time he was to pick up Kay.

When Dane first took command of the hospitals security force he was appalled at the condition of their headquarters. Empty liquor bottles littered both the police side of the building and the small office and garage housing the ambulance and fire apparatus.

He quickly replaced the inefficient men and added others like himself, retired policemen looking for a part time job to augment their pensions.

Their first weeks were spent in training and cleaning up the building. His requests for new office equipment was met with amused smiles by the administrative staff. Using his own funds and attending auctions for used furniture, he was able to secure filing cabinets and a desk to replace the battered equipment he inherited.

His thoughts lately were filled with that of the Teehan woman. As he grew to know her, he learned that she was a gentle, caring person. He had ambivalent feelings when he learned she had two young children. When she first mentioned them, his mind flashed back to that of his own children. He felt a sense of betrayal towards Anna when physical desire for Kay began to grow.

He stared at the ugly green walls and gray steel furniture that reminded him of his first precinct when he was a rookie cop in Brooklyn.

The odor of stale cigarette smoke and strong cleaning antiseptic gave him a headache. As bad as the aroma was, it was better than the air in some of the other buildings of the hospital. Each had its own particular odor. One of the old-timers on his staff told him he could tell what building he was in, even if blindfolded. As an example the geriatric ward smelled strongly of urine, while the drug rehab building reeked with tobacco smoke.

Often, a sweet smell of marijuana would float down the halls of any of the buildings. Dane smiled, this too was not totally unlike some of the precinct houses he had been assigned.

His longshoreman father and his mother were delighted when he passed the test on his 22nd birthday for the police department and positively glowed at his graduation from the police academy. His appointment fulfilled the Irish immigrants' dream for their three sons, one a policeman, another a fireman and the third a priest.

Dane's first assignment was in the picturesque Brooklyn Heights section of the Borough, fifteen minutes from his parents brownstone house. From either location, you could see the famous clock atop the Williamsburg Bank building. The entire borough could see the clock and would set their watches and clocks by its time.

The station house was an ancient building that was once a school but was considered structurally unsafe for children and turned over to the police department. The building's scarred walls had been a hideous green and one of the old timers told him that the battered wooden desks were surplus Army furniture of World War 1 vintage.

He and his friends rollicked in the downtown bars on his beat that his beloved Dodgers used as their playground. That was before they left the borough and took the heart and soul out of Brooklyn.

Jim Dane was marked as an officer with a bright future in front of him. As a rookie he'd made a lucky and important bust of a mafia capo on the waterfront thanks to a tip from his longshoreman father. He later scored high on a Sergeant's test and waited impatiently for the list to come out.

He'd used his good looks and blue uniform to bed any of the groupies he desired that were constantly in the police hangouts.

One night, walking his beat, he found a drunk sleeping on the steps of a brownstone. It had taken Dane only a moment to recognize the man as the Dodger's premier relief pitcher. He brought the man to the Montague hotel where he knew the Dodgers roomed for their home games. The desk clerk gave Dane the number of the pitcher's room and he delivered him to a grateful roommate.

A few nights later he and a friend were off duty and having a drink at The Fisherman's. It was a downtown Brooklyn bar noted for its being a favorite of the Dodgers when in town. A band of men entered the bar and when they asked the bartender for him by name, he identified himself. It was the relief pitcher and several stars of the ball club. Dane and several friends of his from the force and along with a cadre of ballplayers formed a rollicking group that was welcomed anywhere in Brooklyn.

It amazed Dane that the ballplayers were cop mavens who often rode with the men who were assigned to a prowl car. Dane and his friends were given passes to Ebbet's field and would visit the Dodger dressing room after the game when a night on the town was planned. Life was sweet and became complete when he met Anna.

He was an usher in a friend's wedding on Long Island and while recuperating from the wedding reception the next day on the sandy beach, he was introduced to a vision of black hair and alabaster skin in a dazzling white bathing suit. She was tall and slender, with a heart shaped face that was framed by a cap of long, jet black hair and soft brown eyes that reflected a loving, generous nature.

When they shook hands and she smiled, their eyes met and her smile grew warmer.

They arranged to meet that night at a bar overlooking the beach that catered to the young of the area. They danced on the outside deck under the stars to the silky sounds of the Platters and the haunting beauty of A Summer Place. She was as light as a cloud in his arms and when he'd commented on her dancing ability she laughed and told him she danced for a living.

She appeared as a singer-dancer in the musicals in the myriad of playhouses all over Long Island. Anna loved entertaining but the pittance she received from the playhouses forced her to work as a dance instructor in an Arthur Murray studio in nearby Long Beach.

When she was appearing in a musical he saw every performance he could attend, using the complimentary tickets that was part of her wages. Dane marveled at her grace and never failed to be warmed by the smile she gave to he and he alone from the stage.

He courted Anna all summer on the sands of Long Beach and that winter on the magical streets of New York. They were married the following June and had a week's honeymoon in Florida. Anna came to their wedding bed a virgin but her passionate nature made her an amorous, even aggressive partner.

In his sixth year on the force he was selected from the sergeants list and was assigned to the quiet waterfront precinct at the foot of the financial district overlooking the East river.

His children were born a year apart shortly after his promotion to Sergeant, making the circle of contentment around him complete.

Anna wanted him to resign from the force when he was eventually transferred to robbery-homicide in the dangerous Fort Apache in the Bronx. She urged him to transfer to the fire department when she learned that many of his friends on the force were transferring, without losing any of their time served towards retirement.

His brother, by now a battalion chief also pushed him to transfer, pointing out that he could have him immediately placed in a firehouse with many of his friends.

He considered the change seriously when one night he and his driver were roughed up making an arrest of three street thugs on his beat. He and his driver's uniforms had been torn in the struggle and the driver had to go to an emergency room for treatment.

The next morning, the thugs were in court neatly dressed and contrite, their mothers in the front row weeping. The judge, known as "turn me loose Lucy", a notorious liberal, castigated him and the police department and then dismissed the case and released the thugs.

Anna stopped her campaign when seven New York City firemen plunged to a fiery death in an inferno in a downtown warehouse.

They bought a house in the northern section of Suffolk County and Anna was content in her suburban home with their two children.

The loss of Anna and the children left him lonely, bitter, and heavily in the grip of alcohol. He felt that he was unable to protect his family although his profession was to protect people.

Dane was content in his position as Captain of hospital security force but dreaded going home at night to the empty house. Kay was like a sudden appearance of the sun on a cloudy day. Her Julie Andrews like smile seemed to light up a room for him when she entered.

His initial attraction occurred when he heard her throaty, bubbly laugh as he passed a group talking in a hallway. He turned and eyed a pretty, full figured blonde woman. She was almost as tall as he with features a little too broad to be called beautiful. But it was her eyes that enthralled him. He was captivated by her them. They were green but often changed color in different lights.

Their chance meeting at the hospital's annual picnic was the beginning of their romance. They danced, talked and most importantly, laughed the entire day.

He began to look forward to their sharing lunch at the cafeteria as the highlight of his day. Although she was obviously happy to be in his company, he initially found it difficult to ask her for the actual date to go to the play.

Dane picked Kay up in front of her building and they drove the short distance to the restaurant. As they headed for the exit they passed a giant black man walking in the roadway with a broom in his hand. He stopped his lumbering gait and raised the broom in silent salute.

Kay turned as they passed the man, waved and said, "Damn! I left his cigarettes on my desk."

Dane was puzzled.

"His cigarettes?"

"Yeah. His name is June Minney. My first day at work, I met him while he was sweeping the front steps of admission and he scared the hell out of me. He asked me for cigarette and in a panic, I gave him the remains of my pack. From then on, when he sees me driving by, I get a big smile and a wave. Whenever I remember, I bring him a pack. Occasionally I give him chocolate and candy, he particularly loves chocolate bars."

"Doesn't the employee handbook forbid the giving of anything harmful to the patients"

"I mentioned it to his physch and he said it didn't make any difference. It's odd but most of the patients enjoy smoking. It seems to act as a pacifier." She laughed, "He seems to have adopted me. If I'm late leaving the office, he walks me to the car and often will run ahead to hold doors open for me."

Jim viewed the man standing in the road, staring after them, "Just be careful. He's still a patient and Christ, he's as big and solid as a tank."

June Minney stared after the retreating car and began walking after it for a few steps. He halted as the car disappeared around a bend in the road. He muttered softly, "Pretty lady. Good lady."

Minney stopped talking as two patients, seeing him, crossed the road. He rested with his hands on the broom and stared flatly at them until they entered a nearby building.

Minney cocked his head at the sound of children playing wafted over the hospital grounds from the adjacent school. The voices brought back the picture of his school days when the other children would circle him taunting him with words he didn't understand.

The blonde woman was soft looking and always gave him a smile when he walked her to her car at night. He would wait for her by her door tomorrow so that she could smile at him and speak to him in her soft voice. Just like his mam and sissy.

The Old Pier is a popular seafood restaurant located on a bluff overlooking the Long Island Sound. It started out as a tavern catering to the local fishermen. They docked their boats at the end of the day and were met by fish store owners who bought their catch. The owner of the bar would walk the few steps to the dock and buy fish from them before the seafood storeowners would take their entire catch.

The fisherman would then crowd the small bar and the few red tablecloth covered tables were filled by the townspeople. The menu was always the same, catch of the day, huge portions of French fried potatoes and a salad.

When the owner retired to Florida, a Greek couple bought the old tavern and kept the sea ambiance and year by year kept improving and enlarging the restaurant until it had became known as one of the finest dining spots on the Island.

Soon, the decor changed from a rough bar with a few tables to a full blown restaurant. One day, a food critic from the New York Times who was visiting a relative at the hospital, stopped in for dinner.

He thoroughly enjoyed the bluefish, Athenian style and wrote a glowing account of the restaurant. He described the scenery at sunset and it quickly became a favorite of Long Island. When they built a pier to accommodate the yacht crowd, it was impossible to get a table on a weekend. The staff at the hospital who wanted a drink or a meal before heading for home, went to the Old Pier right after work, in order to beat the dinner rush, especially on Fridays.

They arrived at the restaurant early enough to secure a table by the window overlooking the water. The window had an unobstructed view of the sun setting in the sound. The vista was especially spectacular at this time of the year. The sun seemed to be going down between the hundred foot bluffs that guarded the inlet. The sun hitting the water cast a bluish purple haze leading from the Connecticut shore across the water. Ducks, paddled serenely around the boats docked in the inlet.

The big mahogany, parallel shaped bar was filled, mostly with employees of the hospital. They spotted Donna sitting at a corner of the bar and next to her was the stocky police sergeant. He had changed from his uniform into a suit but Donna remained in her white hospital clothes. Donna grinned and saluted them with the drink in her hand as they passed.

Janet, the maitre' d and wife of the owner who was the head chef, escorted them to a table at a window.

Dane picked up his menu, "Did you see how many heads turned around when we came in?"

She nodded, "It looks as though everybody who works in the hospital is here. We'll be an item on Monday."

Dane said, "Your friend, Mrs. Burns works fast. That was the big cop she was with. The one who helped out with that football player this morning."

Kay looked back, "I know. He doesn't look as big without his uniform." Kay looked troubled, "Donna is a great friend and a super lady. She's just lonely and unfortunately makes a mistake with her choice of men now and then. I hope this isn't another one."

"She's a big girl. As for the cop, everybody looks bigger in a uniform. He's probably the same height as me but thirty pounds heavier. He seems alright."

The waitress came and brought the house salad, a huge bowl of fresh lettuce, tomatoes and feta cheese. The dressing was a lightly spiced olive oil and vinegar. A loaf of fresh baked bread was placed next to the salad. Kay ordered a glass of white wine and noted Dane's hesitation before he settled for a glass of white wine. They agreed on the captain's special, a combination of various fresh seafoods.

The salad was delicious and Dane helped himself to a second helping. Kay laughed, "Be careful, the salad is like a siren's song. You'll keep eating it and the bread and not be able to finish the main course."

They were silent for a moment, drinking in the beauty of the sunset. Finally Dane spoke, "I feel a little awkward. This is the first time I've been on a date since my wife died."

She laughed with relief, "Me too. After Donny took off on me, I swore I wouldn't let anybody close to me. When I leave the hospital, I go home to my kids, both of them in going through their terrible teens.

Usually, I'm too tired to even think of going out. On the weekends, the children are active in sports, particularly my son."

"If you don't mind my asking, what happened to your husband?"

A shadow crossed her face, "Our next door neighbor had a live in foreign nanny for their kids." Angered now, "I walked in on them screwing in my bed."

"Where do you stand now?"

"My lawyer tracked him to California. Donny bought himself a dealership in the computer business. The lawyer urged me immediately to get a divorce, but at the time, I know you'll think its stupid, but I didn't want a divorce on religious grounds."

"I don't think that's stupid, but you can't live in the past forever."

"Well anyway, my lawyer had him served with child support papers and he's sending enough to help. Thank God for my sister and her husband. They have been my support loop through all of this. I took this job because it was a perfect fit. I only live a five minute drive from here, but more importantly, the state workers have a great medical plan. I never worried about things such as insurance before, because the family was covered by Donny's company. You can't survive in this country without medical insurance."

She toyed with her salad, "What makes me so mad is how dumb I was. I was only eighteen when we were married. I got pregnant on our honeymoon and had two kids in three years. I later found out he was screwing everything in sight when he was on the road." She bit her lip as she continued, "Thank God for the computer courses I took after the bastard took off."

Dane gently reminded her, "Not all marriages are like that."

She nodded, "I heard that you and your wife were close. Wasn't she awfully young when she died?"

A flicker of pain crossed his features. He drank heavily of the wine before answering, "Anna was only thirty eight. "It's better now, but in the beginning I felt alone on an island of grief and that nobody could understand how I felt. To make matters worse, I started drinking heavily. When I broke my leg on the job, the stay in the hospital and the subsequent rehab left me drink free for the first time since my wife died. As Winston Churchill said, alcohol is a great servant but a terrible master."

"You seem to have it under control."

"I don't think I was ever truly an alcoholic. I take a few glasses of wine now and then but don't have the driving need to keep drinking."

He shook his head and in an apparent attempt to change the subject, "Before I forget, who was that stone faced lady who came into your office this afternoon while we were talking?"

Kay's pretty face made a grimace, "She's one of the phsychs on staff, Paula Farkis. We call her the old bitch, although I don't think she's as old as she looks. For whatever the reason, she resents the younger women and is constantly complaining to our supervisors if we're on the phone with our kids or a few minutes late to work. One of the phsychs told me off the record that she has all the symptoms of a manic depressive. When I first started work here, she was very kind to me, but lately she's been on my case, bringing reports that had to be typed, late in the afternoon and complaining about phone calls from my children."

"Why don't they give her some treatment or get rid of her? Christ, she looks like she should be one of the patients here."

Kay laughed, "The front office and her supervisors would love to, but she's been here for quite a few years and has a lot of seniority."

Quite a few people from the hospital stopped at their table, friends of Kay, who were obviously happy to see her out on a date and curious about the man she was with.

As they were finishing the meal and waiting for coffee, they were interrupted by two men who stopped as they were passing their table. "Hi Kay. I haven't seen you in here before. Who's minding your girls?"

"Hi Bob. My sister is watching them. Jim and I are on our way to the Shakespeare in the Park Festival at the arbortorium."

Dane arose from his chair extending his hand, "I'm Jim Dane. I recently came aboard with the hospital security division."

The two men, still in their white hospital jackets shook hands, "I'm John Abbott and this is Bob Younger." Pointing at an i.d. on his jacket, "We're on the graveyard shift tonight."

Jim sized the two men up, as a man does when faced with possible competition for a woman in whom he has an interest.

The men bore a striking resemblance to each other. Both were tall, over six feet in height with a cap of curly red hair topping a slender frame. The main difference was in their personality which soon manifested itself. Abbot's handshake was vigorous while Younger's shake was soft and limp.

The two men sat down as Kay invited them to join them for a drink. As they were ordering drinks, Dane glanced at the next table and said, "Oh shit."

Kay said, What's wrong?"

"It's that pompous ass of a lawyer that jumped me over the football player the county cops brought in."

Younger looked over at the table and laughed, "I see that you've met our resident asshole. He's a mama's boy who rents a cubbyhole of an office with five other lawyers. He wouldn't have that except that his mommy subsidizes his income and his wife has a hell of a good paying job."

Abbot gulped down his drink, "Screw that jerk. He's got one of the lowest paying jobs in the state. I think he only keeps it to impress the young female aides in the hospital, like the one he's with. He's an intellectual bully and like all bullies, he's a damn coward at heart."

Dane said, "What the hell is a lawyer doing at the hospital?"

Kay looked over at Gunn, "It's a New York State law that every patient is supposed to have a legal advocate to be certain that his civil rights are protected."

Abbott said, "A few of them are conscientious but most of them are like that jerk."

Younger signaled for another round and when the rest of the table shook their heads, he ordered a double. "The thing that really pisses me off is that he's the lead counsel for our resident cannibal."

Dane said, "Our what?"

"He's the guy who castrated, cannibalized and then killed that kid upstate ten years ago. He was found not guilty by reason of insanity and sentenced to life in an upstate mental institution. When they closed it, they sent him here."

Dane was astonished, "And you people are trying to let him go?"

Younger said angrily, "He's a bright guy and came under the care of one of our disciples of Freud. The jerk found him mentally ill but no longer dangerous. Jerk off over there," pointing at Dunn, "heard about it and brought his case to trial. A jury at the county seat agreed with the psyche and declared that he should be set free."

Kay was shaken, "I didn't know that."

"That's because the trial judge set the judgment aside as it didn't fit with the evidence presented at the trial. An appellate ruling granted him a new trial."

Abbott said, "Don't mind him," pointing his thumb at Younger like an umpire calling a batter out on strikes, "he took one of his patients off Prozac and the guy reacted well at first. He had suicidal thoughts while on Prozac and we felt we should try something else. He was put on a temporary suicide watch and as soon as he was free from constant observation, he hung himself. The guy's wife got a lawyer and sued the state for negligence. We got word today from the State Supreme court in Riverhead that the jury just came in and awarded the his wife $250,000.00."

Younger spoke up, "She's also going after me in court. Even if I win, my insurance is going to go through the roof. What kills me is that the son of a bitch acted as sane as anybody here and swore to me that all he wanted was to get home to his wife and kid. The aids on the suicide watch told me the guy seemed happy as hell."

Kay said, "Don't blame yourself. There isn't a test in the world that enables anybody to look into the human mind."

Younger obviously upset, said angrily, "Christ, I'm not blaming myself. It's just that the bastard's wife is now suing me for not taking his psychosis seriously enough."

Abbott spoke to Kay, not looking at Dane. "We're also devastated by the O'Hara girl skipping out. She was one of my patients. We felt that she was responding well to the medication we had been giving her. I told her at our last session that we were considering releasing her as an outpatient. I can't understand the bitch taking off."

Kay was angry, "I can't understand your attitude. I think she was just another kid screwed up by drugs."

Dane leaned back in his chair, "Kay and I have been discussing her. Aren't there an awful lot of young girls taking off?"

Younger looked oddly at Dane, "There's nothing strange about it. Obviously, these girls are all mentally disturbed or they wouldn't be here. Most of them were druggies and used sex to pay for their drug habit. A lot of them continued openly, even in here, to sell themselves for drugs, favors and even cigarettes. They use the grounds, hallways, vacant offices whenever or wherever it suits them. When they feel well enough to leave, most of the girls hop the train to New York and work the streets. I'm sure that's where the O'Hara girl went"

Dane shook his head, "She never took any train out of town. From what I hear, she was a real looker who would have been noticed by the trainmen at that hour of night."

The men rose saying it was time for them to return to the hospital. Kay and Dane watched in silence as the men wended their way through the tables.

Kay felt somewhat responsible about Younger's attitude towards Dane. When she first came to work at the hospital he pressed her to join him on a date. She gently rebuffed him at the time, still hurting from the betrayal of her husband. Intuition told her that there was a tinge of jealously in Younger's actions.

After they left, Kay said, "They've both been good friends to me since I first came to the hospital."

"They're an odd pair. There's so few white doctors on staff that I've seen in the short time I've been here."

Kay shook her head, "They're always together. As a matter of fact, they're both loners and are rarely seen with anybody else." She laughed, "The hospital wouldn't care if they had two heads, they're that short of good doctors. The young ones that the state can snag, hang around only long enough to build up a practice on the side or gain enough experience to join one of the private hospitals. That's why you see so many Asian and Indian doctors. They get a good salary, a house on the grounds and usually a job for their wives. When their twenty years are up, they take their pensions and go back to Asia and live like kings."

Dane changed the subject, "If the O'Hara girl didn't take the train, where is she?"

"She could have hitched a ride to Huntington and caught a train to the city."

Dane shook his head, "I spoke to Nugent, Donna's buddy, about the girl. The O'Hara girl's aunt, an attorney and politically connected, is raising hell with the hospital and the county police about her disappearance. The county assigned a detective, a guy named Dicks, to investigate. He's satisfied that she didn't take a train from here or Huntington that night."

Kay looked around to be certain she wouldn't be overheard, "It's a pretty open secret that there's three young men pushing drugs on the hospital grounds. Someone should talk to the cops about questioning them. The O'Hara girl was pretty tight with them. They may be hiding her."

Dane nodded, "I'll look into it."

They finished their coffee and as they left the restaurant, didn't see the figure with burning eyes watching them from behind a car at the bottom of the parking lot.

⇒ Chapter 7

After the incident with the Wainwright girl and being seen by the professor, Drack heavily sedated himself for the entire weekend. He was preparing to leave his office late Monday when Belial's silky voice startled him. He ordered Drack to go to the admissions building where the Teehan woman was working late finishing up the heavy influx of the day's new patients. It would be a simple matter to drag her to the tunnel and back to the collection room. There they could work on her, slowly.

Drack no longer tried to ignore the voices, and with the heat in his body rising, with the thought of having the woman in his trophy room, he went to the stairwell and hurried down to the basement where the old root cellar had been.

Drack slid a surgical knife into his belt, and flicked on a flashlight as they entered the tunnel. Belial floated ahead leading the way with a silent Lew at his side.

Red O'Dwyer stepped into the New York Hotel bar, his blue eyes squinting with effort to adjust to the gloom after coming in from the bright afternoon sun. His long red hair was unkempt and badly needing a trimming.

The hotel was located just past the parking lot of the train station and relied heavily on the commuters who stopped in for a drink after their long train ride from the city.

Two men seated at the bar turned at his entrance and the bartender looked up from his paper. Red slid onto the stool next to Tommy Izzo whose eyes never left his reflection in the mirror behind the bar. Tommy would sit at a bar staring intently at himself for hours, pausing only long enough to take a sip from his drink.

Periodically, he would run a comb carefully through his long black hair, eyes never leaving his reflection. The only people he was ever seen speaking to were his girl Dolly, Red and Frankie Carroll. The four of them were tied together through the common bond of drugs.

Red ordered a beer and waited until the bartender had moved back to his paper before asking, "Did you get it?"

Tommy simply nodded and pointed to a pair of plastic shopping bags on the floor of the bar next to his stool.

Red hid his exasperation at the man's silence, not wanting to offend Tommy, who had a violent temper but more importantly had connections all over the Island to a variety of drugs.

He glanced furtively at the other man sitting at the bar and recognized him as one of the tenants of the hotel who, like the other residents, spent his days and nights between his room and the bar. He rarely left the hotel except to cash his monthly pension check. The man was in a drunken stupor staring at his glass oblivious to his surroundings.

Relieved, Red turned to Tommy, "Great! As soon as Frankie comes in with the booze, lets book and go some place where we can cut the stuff. I'm damned near broke. Then we'll party."

Tommy nodded, "Lets not overdo the party bullshit. I need money just as badly as you do. When we cut the shit, we'll tour the school grounds and locate some of our customers looking for a hookup."

Red nodded and as if on cue, Frankie staggered through the door clutching a shopping bag in one hand and with his shoes tied together and hung around his neck. When Frankie was drunk, he took his shoes off, claiming that his feet were swollen and the shoes hurt his feet.

When the bartender refused to serve Frankie the drink he ordered, he reached into the shopping bag and brought out a bottle of bourbon. Staring defiantly at the bartender he began drinking straight from the bottle.

"Red, get him the hell out of here," nodding towards Frankie and his brown sack, and pointing to the shopping bags, "and take that shit with you. Blackie the cop knows you three are pushing and told me to keep you out of here or he'll take my license. Legal age or not, he don't want you in any of the bars in Queens Park. He don't want you guys in town. Period!."

The three young men stood outside the bar debating where to go to divide the drugs. Their first chore was to cut the coke and marijuana and put them into plastic sandwich bags for resale.

When they sold the drugs it would give them more than enough profit to recoup their outlay and leave ample cash to make their next buy. Even then, there would be plenty of cocaine left to support their growing habit.

Red's suggestion that they go to Tommy's room above the bar was met with an emphatic shake of the head, "Blackie knows I live there. He's such a fucking hard ass, he'll go there today for sure. Besides, Dolly's up there sleeping one off. I don't want her to know about this until we have it cut."

Frankie giggled, "I know where to go. The maintenance building at the hospital is perfect."

The other two looked at each other, Red objecting, "Are you crazy? There are enough people working there that know us. We'll have cops all over our asses and besides, the nuts in that place give me the creeps."

Frankie took the bottle of Jack Daniels from the bag and drank heavily from it, "It's after four-thirty. Everybody will be gone from the place by now. They start leaving at two thirty and the rest of the buildings are emptied out by now. If you stand in the doorway of any of those buildings at this time of day, you'll get killed in the stampede."

Red shrugged, looked at Tommy who nodded agreement and said, "All right, we'll get my car and drive over and park the car on Williams Road and walk the rest of the way in. We can't go through town with you carrying your shoes around your neck and a bag full of booze."

Red looked at Tommy, "You're packing, aren't you?"

He nodded and patted his side pocket, "I'm glad I brought it along. If any of those nuts bother us, I'll take care of them."

They drove to the hospital without incident and Frankie led Red and Tommy through the deserted maintenance building and down into the basement.

A few months earlier he was prowling the grounds looking for something to steal to help pay for a hit. He found a side door that was usually left unlocked by the men who did general repair work for the hospital. He went down to the basement and found a door behind some canvas. He forced it open and ventured only a few feet into the darkness. When it looked like it was only an empty storage room he traveled no farther.

———————

He led them to the basement and through the door into the storage room. The three were giggling from the bourbon they were sipping as they walked to the hospital.

Tommy, his thin body shivering from the damp, "Lets build a fire from that old lumber in the corner."

Red agreed saying, "We'd better move as far away from the door as possible. We don't want to set off the smoke alarms upstairs."

They gathered some lumber and moved towards the shadows of the rear of the room. To their surprise, rounding a corner they found a long passageway that extended beyond the range of their flashlights.

They went a good distance into the tunnel until the impatience for a drink became too strong to resist. Using the paper bags they used to transport the bourbon and beer, they quickly turned the lumber into a roaring fire. The smoke drifted up the passageway, and away from them. They settled down and began cutting the coke with a mixture of flour and sugar into dime bags made from plastic sandwich sacks and weighing each bag on a small postage scale.

When they finished with the cocaine, Tommy picked up a small brick of marijuana and they quickly split it up, still being careful not to use any of the drugs while they were working, taking small sips of the bourbon instead. When they were finished, they settled back, looking at a small hill of filled plastic bags.

Red smiled a wolfish grin, "This is our biggest score yet. We must have over ten grand in profit sitting here."

Tommy nodded, his tongue finally loosened by the alcohol, "We should be able to unload all of it in a week to the high school kids. Not a bad week's pay."

The two quickly loaded the drugs into a garbage bag. Red drank deeply from the bottle, "I wonder where the hell Mary Theresa went. I'd love to have her here with us now."

Tommy watched Red as he dipped into a bag of coke with a spoon and snorting it, "Why worry about her? Every day they bring in more fresh, young cunt to the hospital looking for a hook up. You're like a cat in a room full of mice, afraid that one of them is going to get away from you. Be like Frankie and enjoy yourself."

They looked at Frankie, passed out and snoring, laughed, and started to party.

Chapter 8

Drack approached a fork in the passageway and was about to take the turn to the right that would lead him to the admissions building. His flashlight cut the inky blackness that covered him except for the dim light that filtered down from one of the many air vents above ground over the tunnel.

The flashlight would surprise an occasional rat, as big as a cat, it's red eyes staring defiantly at him before insolently moving into a hole in the wall.

Drack stiffened as a few tendrils of smoke floated up around his nostrils and up through one of the vents. Belial and Lew beckoned him to the left fork towards the smoke. Their figures blended in with the blackness, making it impossible at times for Drack to see them.

Suddenly, he heard laughter and he saw a light in the distance. He stopped and drew the knife from his belt before continuing. Some one was in his tunnels.

Red and Tommy finished packing the drugs away in the plastic bags except for a small bit of the marijuana. This, they expertly rolled into cigarettes, lit up, and were content to lean back smoking, occasionally nipping at the bourbon. The fire burned down to a small blaze, the thin wisps of smoke mixing with the sweet odor of the marijuana. The fire was enough to warm them against the damp cold of the catacombs, but had withdrawn it's light from the tunnel behind it.

Red blinked his eyes and gasped unbelievingly as a tall figure suddenly appeared behind the fire, a white coat covering his body from neck to knees.

Tommy heard the intake of breath and looked up in a drugged haze at the tall figure standing silently, "What are you looking at, you asshole? If you want a hook up, come across with some cash or get the hell out of here."

Red giggled, "I know who he is. He's one of the doctors from the hospital. I saw him grab Peggy by the tits the other day. She gave him the bird and took off."

The figure stood motionless and silent, his features hidden by shadows, as Tommy rose unsteadily to his feet, and struggled to get the pistol from his pocket. "I don't give a shit who he is. I think he's seen too much to leave here, I'm going to turn him into fish bait."

As Tommy brought the gun up and hastily fired, the figure in white leaped at him his arm raised and extended from it was the brightest knife Tommy had ever seen. He had time for one horrified scream as the knife flashed in a shimmer of light.

Red, halfway to his feet and still in a kneeling position stared unbelievingly as Tommy fell, his head severed almost completely from his body.

Red pulled frantically at his pocket for the knife they used to cut the coke, but knew he was moving too slow to escape as the killer sprang at him. He was able to free the knife and then found his hand encased in a powerful grip. He thought he was punched in the chest until he saw the blood gushing from his body. He died instantly with the second blow.

The sound of the shot aroused Frankie long enough to realize that his friends were dead around him and something was kneeling over him. A hand grabbed him by the hair and slashed downward. He didn't know he was dying when the hand came down again in an arc.

⇒ Chapter 9

After the killings in the catacombs, Drack fled back to his home carrying the huge supply of drugs he found at the scene. The resistance of the victims, and the bullet that grazed his side left him shaken. Their long hair and the near darkness fooled him into thinking they were three young girls. The fact that he was careless enough to have been recognized being with the Wainwright slut completely alarmed him. Drack steeled himself against the thought of having to go back that night and bring the bodies out to a burial ground. They were the first males he killed and killing them did not give him the sexual warmth of taking a woman.

He had no interest in taking a trophy from them but was elated to find the plastic bag full of drugs. Although he felt no remorse about the killing, he was intrigued about the possible benefit of the huge supply of drugs he took from the scene. It was pure impulse since he hadn't experimented with cocaine since his younger days in college.

He put his bloodied hospital gown in a plastic bag and left it in the basement. As usual, he would take it to the incinerator later that night. He checked the bullet wound and found that it had put an angry red furrow along his side with very little bleeding. He sterilized the wound and put a bandage over it and vowed to be more careful in the future.

71

It was Belial that suggested that it was better, when possible, to take his victims to his collection room for the sacrifice and the taking of his trophy. The ritual was best performed with Drack completely naked and the music of Wagner competing with the screams of his victims. When he was finished, his body would be dyed red with the blood of the victim. More importantly was the feeling that he experienced when the victims saw him nude. The terror in their eyes and their screams of pain when he began to take them was unbelievable. His orgasms were the best at these times.

He dosed himself heavily with Prozac and began to experiment with small hits of cocaine. The euphoria of the cocaine gave him a sense of power and filled him with the feeling that he could kill anyone that got in his way. Male or female.

The combination enabled him to control the voices and he moved about the hospital on his rounds for a week with a half smile that puzzled those who knew him.

Then disaster struck. A surprise audit of the pharmaceutical closet in the Central Supply building revealed a startling shortage of narcoleptic drugs. There was a small supply of the drugs kept in a cabinet for emergency purposes on the floors of the violent wards and shortages were also reported.

Until now, Drack was content with the narcoleptic drugs and didn't bother with the cocaine he found in the cabinets when legally filling a prescription for a patient.

Stringent security measures were put into effect on all the drug supply cabinets. The hospital security force conducted an investigation and he was listed as one of the Doctors with the most requests listed in the journal in the drug closet.

He was closely questioned as to its use, but was able to satisfy the investigators. However, he was unable to replace his dwindling supply of Prozac and had to take small doses until he could gain access to another source. To make up for the loss of the hospital supply, he began to rely heavily on the cocaine he found with the three men in the tunnel. He rapidly became dependant on the drug.

The scarlet, mocking face of Belial appeared suddenly to Drack while he was preparing for the quarterly treatment meeting scheduled for the following morning.

He sneered, "We haven't seen you lately. Do you think you are done with us? Come, it is time we complete the sacrifice of that Teehan slut."

Drack nodded meekly, the killing of the Teehan woman had become an obsession with Belial. He immediately arose from his desk and went into the catacombs. Belial and Lew led the way underground, unerringly to the admissions building. When they arrived at the door leading into the building, Drack cautiously opened it and peered into the basement. There was no one about and all seemed quiet. It was past four thirty, and the day shift had already left.

They quietly mounted the stairs and headed for Kay's office where the grinding sound of a computer printer broke the silence of the empty hospital hall.

As they silently made their way toward the woman, a car door slammed that drew their attention to the main entrance. Dane was just mounting the steps into the building. Fear of the man drove Drack back towards the door to the catacombs. The fear was replaced by hatred as he fled with a screaming Belial and Lew urging the sacrifice of both Kay and Dane.

A shaken Drack fled fearfully back down to the catacombs and to safety. His experience with the men in the tunnel made him cautious towards taking male victims.

The participants in the treatment meeting were divided into four groups. First were the medical doctors easily identified by the stethoscopes hanging from their neck and the expensive suits they wore. Most were oriental or of Indian descent and only a few were women. Through the din of the conversation and cigarette smoke, there were few smiles.

The Orientals were dressed in the fashion of the successful Japanese businessmen with black suits and snowy white shirts. The Indians copied the Japanese slavishly in dress ever since they exploded onto the world's economic stage. They secretly relished in delight as the Japanese supplanted the Americans in economic areas around the world.

The second group next to them were the Psychiatrists who oddly enough were all Caucasian and almost half were feminine. The conversations among them were studied and deliberate and all wore the same grave stare. Their dress was casual with most clad in a sport coat and slacks.

A third group, the nurses and therapy aids, were clustered together standing out with their crisp white uniforms. They were a relaxed, noisy group with a gentle laughter emanating from them, secure in the knowledge that they were the real driving force of the hospital.

The last group was the social workers, all female and all dressed in a uniform of their own, in business suits and carrying leather attaché cases. They were the smallest group and clustered tightly together with little conversation and much examination of wristwatches.

The treatment team leader, Dr. Charles Liebman nervously banged the gavel calling the meeting to order. The assembled staff halted their somber discussion on the latest rounds of personnel cuts ordered by Albany.

Doctor Liebman, a short rotund man with a round face, his glasses continually sliding down his button nose, addressed the staff, "For those of you attending your first treatment team meeting, I'll briefly cover the format. We'll cover six patients today by reviewing their case histories. Each of you will have a duplicate of the reports of the last group of assessments on each patient. These reports were written by a member of each profession here. After I have read the report, the meeting will be open for comments or questions."

He glanced up, pushing his glasses up on his nose, "The first patient, Richard Olsen, had been progressing and was released to Option house, a halfway house on the grounds, with unsupervised visits to his home in Huntington. Recently he was re-admitted back into Building 23, a secure facility, because of progressive deterioration in his condition. This was brought about by a relapse into the use of crack/cocaine and alcohol abuse. He was missing program events at the halfway house and staying in bed pondering suicide. He dyed his hair black and is hearing voices again, which in his case is a particularly serious danger sign, since one of the voices he claims he hears is the devil urging him to violent actions."

He looked up in annoyance as two latecomers entered the hall, "His parents refuse to have him live at home on his weekend passes because of his increasing tendency towards violence. His mother told Doctor Paul that she feared for her life and that of his siblings on his last visit. Richard is 27 and has a long history of psychiatric illness and alcohol and drug abuse. He has been a patient at Queens Park for the past five years. He has been repeatedly diagnosed as schizophrenic and has in the past continually had symptoms of auditory hallucination, delusive thinking and dysphonic mood withdrawal. Richard belonged to a satanic cult during his adolescence but denies any interest in Satanism at present. His medical health is excellent with no allergies."

The doctor halted long enough to take a drink of water and allow the staff to finish their notes, "His history of chemical abuse began when he was fifteen with marijuana and alcohol and increasing to and including crack/cocaine. His current mental status is poor. Richard dresses appropriately casual and is neat and clean. He is outwardly cooperative except when he is hearing voices. At these times his face will contort into a bizarre facial expression and lately will attack anyone near him without provocation. He is unable to remain still. As an example, when sitting, both legs will jiggle continuously. He lies without reason and is only truthful to questions to which he feels I know the answers. He has little to no insight into his true condition. His recent and remote memory are intact, which is remarkable considering the heavy drug abuse. He is a chronic MICA patient and when abusing drugs is easily led, subject to outside suggestion and is manipulative and violent."

Kay, who was taking notes, interrupted Liebman, "Excuse me doctor, I don't recognize the term. Did you say mica?"

"It's MICA in capitals. It means a patient with a dual diagnosis wherein he is mentally and clinically dependant. Now to continue, prognosis is a continuation of his present pattern and a lifetime dependency on care from a mental health facility. The treatment team's recommendation is continued Narcoleptic and other psychotropic drug therapy. He needs individual as well as group psychotherapy and strong substance abuse counseling."

Here the doctor paused nervously, "He has had unusually violent side effects to Prozac and it is strongly recommended that his file be such noted. This report is signed by Doctors Paul, Harris, Younger and primary therapist Paula Farkis with exceptions. Our recording secretary today is Mrs. Kay Teehan. She won the job because she is one of the few secretaries at the hospital that is able to take shorthand." Amidst a gentle wave of laughter, "Any comments or suggestions?"

A sea of hands were raised immediately, "Dr. Younger, why don't you lead off. I know that you had some exceptions to the report."

Younger stood up, his red hair neat except for a forelock that hung down on his forehead and read from prepared notes. "I disagree with the emphasis on Olsen's predilection for violence. When I had him on Klonopin and gave him individual therapy, he was interacting very well with people in his residence. He was even elected president of his community residence. With the aid of controlled drugs, he was alcohol and crack free for three months. As for his attacking anybody, he hasn't harmed anybody in three years. I recommend he be put back on an aggressive Klonipan treatment and allowed to stay at the Options house. By the way, I was the Physician that prescribed Prozac for Olsen. I don't think we should rule out its use for him until further study. He was still being given other antidepressants and it's possible that the combination caused the violent reaction."

The therapy treatment leader, Dr. Karpis, her sallow face expressionless arose, "I agree with Doctor Younger. The Olsen boy doesn't represent a danger to anybody. We're under constant pressure from Albany to clear our wards and now they reduce our staff and close more wards twice a year. If we can free patients like Olsen, it will enable our people to concentrate on our sicker patients, particularly those who are a danger to society and those with multiple personality disorders."

The last comment raised a hubbub of noise, with Harris speaking without rising, "I realize that multiple personality disorders had become the "in thing" in mental illness, but we still have a load of people with other serious illnesses under our care. We should move slower, not faster in releasing these patients."

Farkis broke into the din, "We can no longer coddle patients like Olsen with our shortage of people and limited resources. We also have to realize that we cannot be a shelter for the homeless and the aged who have historically signed themselves in here under the guise of mental illness."

Doctor Harris arose, blue eyes cold with anger, "I can't believe you are recommending less control over Olsen on one hand and admitting that he is dangerous. What you're also suggesting is that we dump helpless people on the streets with nowhere to go and who have definite mental problems, however minor they may be. Most of the homeless are mentally ill. We have patients here for thirty years who fit that category. If we push them out into the streets, they'll die."

He waved his hands to quiet the audience as he continued, "For Christ's sake, everyone in this room has had an incident where he's almost run over a patient walking along the hospital grounds. Yesterday, on my way back from lunch, a patient suddenly decided to cross the road in front of me. Fortunately, I had time to stop and avoid hitting him. How many will be killed in the normal traffic in the outside world?" Amidst an uncomfortable silence, he continued, "As for Richard Olsen, I consider him an extremely risky case. He's hearing voices that are talking to him of murder and sacrifice. If you release him as an out-patient, I greatly fear that he will kill someone."

Farkis, still standing, broke the silence of the room, "When he is under psychotropic treatment he is almost normal. We can handle up to a third of our patients like him as outpatients. With the closing of two more buildings in the fall, we simply have no other choices."

Harris spoke again, "The outpatient system doesn't work. These people forget to come in for their treatment and eventually go some place to die. Or you'll have incidents such as the Schnabel and Fusco cases."

There wasn't a sound in the room. George Schnabel had been a patient in the Upslip facility on the south shore of the Island. He was put in the violent ward of the hospital and while under drug treatment, was a gentle, cooperative patient with one exception. He repeatedly said to anyone who would listen, that the minute he was released he was going to immediately go home and kill his wife. Despite the written warnings in his file from the judge, detective, and prosecuting attorney on his case and the physiatrist who had originally had him committed, a foolish and arrogant doctor ignored the warnings and released him on a weekend pass one Friday afternoon.

Schnabel made good his threat and within a half an hour of his release broke into his house and stabbed his wife to death in front of their terrified children.

Fusco was a brilliant Professor of mathematics at a State University who slowly drifted into insanity and was one of the first patients released under the new austerity program. He was to be treated as an outpatient on Prozac. Two hours after his release, he was captured in the city after pushing a woman in front of a subway train.

The news media had a field day with the two incidents, fanning cries of outrage from the public. Two of the city dailies ran a series of uncomplimentary articles on the mental hospitals in New York State.

The psychiatrist who signed the release for Fusco angrily shouted from the back of the room, "I had no choice but to release Fusco. The State Mental Hygiene Legal group forced me to release him. Those goddamn lawyers think that a law degree gives them a godlike status. Besides, nobody will ever convince me that you can prove any links between Prozac and behavior similar to Fusco. Not without extensive clinical trials."

Doctor Liebman, whose prime qualification to be in the position he held, was his marriage to the sister of the chief of service at the hospital, held up his hands unhappily, "Gentlemen, gentlemen, we are getting away from our patient. Dr. Paul, we haven't heard from you today." He looked over the room and when he couldn't see him repeated, "Dr. Paul?"

Dr. Harris looked at his neighbor, Dr. Paul who was sound asleep in the chair. He reached out and pushed the man gently at first and when he didn't wake from his alcoholic haze, he shook him roughly. The man was a brilliant physiatrist who was originally able to contain his drinking to the weekends. The weekends expanded to include Fridays and Mondays until he now drank steadily every day. On the last shove from Harris, he struggled to his feet, gray hair awry, stammered, "Yes I agree."

The audience smiled, some laughed loudly. Liebman simply said "Thank you Dr. Paul." and the doctor sat down looking around in his fog. Liebman ignored the condition of Dr. Paul. If he made an issue and a report was submitted, he would lose a doctor that would not be replaced.

"We have five other cases to cover today. I recommend we continue the Olsen case until our next treatment meeting. I suggest that Doctor Younger be his primary physiatrist and Dr. Farkis his treatment leader and they should submit a report at that time. Meanwhile he should be moved back to Options house where he seemed to thrive."

The rest of the cases were quickly handled and as the meeting was filing out, Kay fell into step with Harris who said with a troubled look, "I have no doubt that one day Olsen will obey those voices he's hearing and act on them."

The crowd in the hallway waiting for the elevator were stunned into silence as a patient known by the staff as the professor came shambling into view and after staring wide eyed at the emerging crowd, gave a terrified shriek and fled the building.

⇒ Chapter 10

The Monday after the monthly treatment meeting, an aide came back from vacation in Pennsylvania, loaded down with boxes of fresh blueberries and put a pint on the desk of everyone in Admissions. Coming into Kay's office he gave her a pint and explained that on his way back from the Poconos, he made a side trip to visit a friend in New Egypt, NJ. He became lost and wound up in the blueberry bog section of New Jersey, just outside the Great Pines area.

Drack was in Kay's office picking up some papers on a newly arrived patient. The mention of the area he was born in gave him an involuntary start. He hadn't thought about New Egypt or the farm in years.

That afternoon he cautiously called the Robinson farm, the family who took him in after the murders of his family and the destruction of the coven. To insure privacy, Drack used the pay phone in the local library. He was fortunate to reach the slow witted son, Ed, instead of the boys parents. The man told him that the County Public Administrator, a close friend of Drack's father was searching for him. Drack's uncle had died in Rahway prison and the administrator just learned that Drack's father had recently died and that Drack was the sole surviving heir. If he didn't come in to claim the property, the two farms would be sold at an auction and the funds would be given to the state. Property values had soared in the area and the land was worth a fortune. Drack told Robinson to tell the administrator he was alive and would be in touch.

Drack hung up the telephone and pondered his situation. As far as he could see there was no danger to him or Ed would have said something.

The library had a desk that contained out of state telephone books for adjoining states. He looked up a law firm in Bordentown in the New Jersey book. He called the firm and spoke to one of the members. Drack was told he needed to send them a letter of authorization and identification so that they could begin working on his claim.

That night Drack sent off the necessary papers and a check to cover legal fees.

Kay and Donna sat at a picnic bench on the boardwalk and patiently waited for Dane and Pat Nugent to arrive. The late fall sun was warm enough so that they could enjoy the beach scenery in comfort. They came to the state park every sunny day and carried their lunches with them. The regulars on the boardwalk nodded to them and smiled at the two attractive woman who looked like sisters.

Kay hesitating, asked Donna, "How serious are you and Pat."

Donna was caught with her sandwich halfway to her mouth, she stared for a moment at Kay before answering, "He's going to leave his wife and move in with me. Don't look so shocked, he's made me the happiest I've been since my husband died."

"What about his family?"

"They're all married and out of the house. He and his wife have been married in name only for quite a few years."

They sat silently for a few moments each with their thoughts, watching the joggers running by and the anglers on the beach, surf casting. Kay broke the silence, "Donna, I don't want to be prying, but if you two care for each other, why don't you get married."

"Because the Nugents are Catholic. He would go for the divorce but she is deeply religious and won't go that route."

Kay laughed, "If Sister Mary Margaret could hear this conversation, she would say we were both going straight to hell."

Donna said testily, "You Catholics with your hang-ups. How in the world can you live under the laws of a bunch of old men in Rome?"

Kay answered defensively, "They aren't all laws of the Catholic church. We live in a Judeo/Christian society that are supposed to live under a set of rules that is designed to protect the institution of the family."

Donna softened her tone, surprised at Kay's reaction,

"Religion is the smallest part of our problem. Our main troubling issue is financial."

Kay looked puzzled, "I thought you were well off and just worked here to keep busy and surely he makes enough money as a police sergeant."

"We'll have plenty of money to retire on but there's a lot of problems as to my estate. Pat is ten years older than me and the way the laws are now, if in the future, he goes into a long term illness, it could wipe me out. There wouldn't be anything for me to live on and I couldn't leave my kids anything."

"There must be some way around that. Perhaps, long term health care insurance?"

Donna shook her head, "It's too expensive. We've checked with lawyers and accountants and the only solution is to co-habit. That's legalese for shacking up. The lawyer told us that's why you see so many elderly people getting divorced when one of the spouses gets seriously ill and needs nursing home care."

Kay said, "We don't have that problem. Poor Dane lost all his immediate family and that bastard Donny didn't leave me a cent," she laughed, "If someone told me fifteen years ago that I would be married and having an affair and my best friend calmly told me she was going to move in with a married man, I'd have told them they were crazy."

Donna said nothing and as they saw Dane and Pat approaching, they discarded their garbage and arose to meet them.

The next day was the forensic committee meeting. Only selected members of the psychiatric staff had to attend but interested medical personnel were also welcome. Dr. Liebman was in Albany at a conference and Dr. Abbott chaired the meeting.

Dr. Abbott opened the meeting promptly at nine o'clock. "Good morning. We have as our guest speakers today, Dr. David Scheman who is a Professor of Genetics at Stanford University and Dr. Albert Guiness of Cold Spring Harbor Laboratory which as you know is located right here on Long Island. They are currently working together with Johns Hopkins University on genetic links to manic depression. Dr. Scheman will be our first speaker."

Dr, Scheman was a stocky, balding man with piercing blue eyes. "Thank you for inviting us here today. I am on a working vacation and spending some time at the Cold Spring Harbor Research facility with my colleague, Dr. Guiness. We have just been given a three million dollar grant by the Charles Dana foundation." He held up his hands for silence as the group applauded the announcement. "This will greatly facilitate the exchange of ideas between our Stanford, Cold Spring Harbor and you folks. We are the three institutions who seem to be leading the way in this country for our work in the neuroscience field.

It has already enabled us to have a computer program written especially for us to network between the three centers. Dr. Guiness felt that we could spend some time with you and perhaps pick up some cases of families with a history of manic depression that we could research. That is of course if the families of those patients who fit our parameters are willing to help."

The audience was silent, listening in rapt attention, until surprisingly, Dr. Paul spoke up, "I did some work while I was a post Doctorate fellow at Cal Tech. I know that at the time you people were working on how genes were structured. Is this an outgrowth of this research?"

As Doctor Paul sat down, his colleagues were stunned. No one at the hospital were aware that the alcoholic doctor had such a heavy scientific background.

Dr. Guiness responded, "An excellent question. The nature of human genome, for you people who are not in our field, is the set of genes used in building the human body. We are positive that genes play a significant role in psychiatric illness."

Dr. Abbott interjected, "That's why we have the question on our admission papers as to whether or not a patient's family had a history of mental illness."

Dr. Scheman nodded, "The human genome includes about 80,000 genes. Our recent breakthrough in DNA research is allowing us to collect data that should speed our research. When we find out why a gene becomes "broken", we'll learn how to fix it and drugs such as Prozac, that we originally thought was fire stolen from the gods will merit just a few paragraphs in any book on pharmacology."

A psychiatrist stood and angrily said, "Hold on. We don't hand out our pills like candy at Halloween. We get all kinds of mental patients in here. We don't know what the hell goes on in their minds all the time. But, Prozac and the other drugs work. At least they do help a significant number of people to get out into the world and lead normal lives. In particular, we have seen dramatic changes in our violent patients."

Dr. Scheman held up his hands in a defensive position, "Whoa, I'll amend that. Until we find out why and what genes pass on abnormality from generation to generation, of course you'll have to fight with what tools you have. This includes the drugs you are using now and of course surgery."

"You mean Lobotomy and Cingulotomy?"

One of the medical doctors asked, "What the hell is Cingulotomy?"

Dr. Scheman hesitated, "It's used only in a limited parameter. I know you folks are using Lobotomy, in fact the entire profession is taking another look at this as an option. We have seen some excellent results of lobotomy in our violent patients." Then looking at the Doctor who asked about the Cingulotomy, "To answer your question, Cingulotomy is a fairly recent breakthrough which has been useful in helping people with Obsessive Compulsive Disorder. Quite a few patients with OCD who have the usual symptoms of bizarre facial tics or suddenly jumping up and down have been cured by this procedure. A surgeon will deliberately damage the cingulata which is located in the limbic region of the brain by piercing it with a long thin electrode. The limbic region appears to play an important role in controlling some of the senses, notably, sadness, fear and pleasure."

Dr. Abbott who was standing alongside of Dr. Scheman and listening intently said, "I've heard of the procedure but will not recommend it for any of my patients. No one really understands why this procedure works and its success ratio is only about forty percent." He slowly shook his head, "Too many people still have the idea that surgery on the brain is a picture of Dr. Frankenstein running amok in our asylums. If word got out that we are doing an operation that we're not sure of, it will set our profession back twenty years."

Dr. Younger added, "What scares the hell out of me is the damaging of the part that controls pain, pleasure and fear. We could be making an insane robot who kills without fear or pleasure. But I appreciate the sharing of ideas. It can only help. But frankly, this procedure applies to maybe ten percent of our patient population. Most of the patients we are seeing now are the results of drug abuse. Anyone who says that he knows what's going on in their minds when they turn violent is naive. The Manson family is perfect examples of this."

Dr. Guiness held his hands up to quiet the murmuring of agreement from the assembly, "We are not here to recommend any changes in your treatment methods. All we ask is that you join us in an exchange of ideas. We all have the interests of the mentally ill at heart. In closing our share of the meeting, I would like to point out that the first OCD patient was Shakespeare's Lady Macbeth who was constantly washing her hands. Friend Willy could have been our first Psychiatrist."

As the visiting guests sat down to laughter and applause Dr. Paul stood, "I'm glad that you brought that example up because lately I have been leaning away from Freudian Psychology as a primary cure for all serious brain disorders."

Dr. Farkas broke into the stunned silence, "That's nonsense. Our profession has been curing mental illness since Freud hit this country in the beginning of this century with the "talking cure." Are you repudiating everything we've learned since then?"

Looking uncomfortable, Dr. Paul shook his head, "No, I'm not suggesting any such thing. But what these gentlemen are suggesting is that before Freud's teaching was hijacked by members of our profession, it was the accepted belief that the most severe disorders were biologically based."

There was an angry clamor from the audience and Dr. Abbott rose, his hands held out as if to clam the noise, "I think we should consider all we've heard here today. After all, our profession is based upon talking and listening. We have other items on the agenda we have to get to and it's getting late."

After the meeting ended, the visiting scientists walked out of the room with Dr. Abbott and the rest of the doctors. Dr. Scheman said, "Your Dr. Paul seems to have ideas that are beginning to spread into our profession."

Dr. Abbott nodded, "I can't say that I agree with him totally, but there are some things he brought up with which I concur."

As the group left the building, the professor was walking by and upon seeing them, began running.

⇒ Chapter 11

Drack arrived at his office immediately after the monthly forensics meeting, shaken once again by the professors reaction to him. He was fascinated by the cingulatory procedure and its possibility of legally getting a patient on an operating table.

As he was going through his mail, he discovered a letter from the law firm in Bordentown, advising Drack that they successfully filed a claim for the estate in his name. A title search was completed that showed the property to be unencumbered and that it was imperative for him to come in to their offices so that he could sign the necessary papers in order to complete his claim.

The thought of leaving his house for that long a time terrified him. It would be the first time that he would be absent from the house for any length of time since he joined the hospital. He always spent any time off including his vacations, secluded in his house. He was only away once when he was forced to go on an overnight trip when a seminar on mental health was held that he had to attend.

Claiming a family emergency, he asked for and received a week of his vacation. He called the lawyers and agreed to an appointment at their offices for the following Monday.

Meanwhile, he was careful to avoid any contact with the professor since his hysterical reaction after the treatment meeting. He was confident that the time away from the hospital would erase from the professor's mind the scene of his taking the Wainwright girl. For safety's sake he would have to eventually deal with the professor.

Kay and Dane spent every free moment together. They took day trips with Kay's children who at first eyed Dane with open hostility and suspicion. On their first trip, they rode the Orient Point Ferry across the Long Island sound into Mystic Seaport and visited the atomic submarine base in Connecticut. Kay's daughter seemed to be warming up but the boy remained aloof.

Other Sundays, they journeyed into the city and visited the Statue of Liberty and the Empire State building. Dane was astonished that neither of the children had ever visited the city and that Kay had only been there twice.

The Sunday trips to the city, the tours of the famous sights and an occasional matinee to a Broadway play, fascinated the children. They particularly enjoyed seeing the famous Mime, Marcel Marceau at the Danny Kaye Theater at Hunter College.

Kay was troubled by her son's continued reaction to Dane and explained, "Little Don adored his father and won't admit that he abandoned them. They hunted and fished together and both enjoyed football. Give it time. He'll come around."

Slowly the girl began to soften her stance towards Dane. Privately, Dane thought that Don was spoiled and would never come around. In truth, he didn't like the boy but hid the feeling from Kay.

Kay was enthusiastic on the visit to the city and to see the famous landmarks that heretofore she saw only on television. She explained to Dane that her husband hated going into the city. It was after one such trip when Kay and Dane made love for the first time.

Kay was preparing dinner at her house when his pager went off. He used her phone to call the hospital and came back into the kitchen with an unhappy look on his face, "That was the office. Mike Dowling has the weekend duty and just called in sick. They can't reach his backup, so I'm elected."

Kay was disappointed, both children had plans for the night and she was looking forward to a romantic evening together, "Can't you at least wait until you've eaten dinner?"

He shook his head, "There isn't anyone on duty right now and my contract calls for me to fill in when a situation like this arises. I'll grab a sandwich on the way and make a pot of coffee at the station."

"Why don't I make a dish up for the both of us and I'll bring it over as soon as the kids eat and leave. We can nuke it at the station house and have dinner together."

"That would be terrific."

Later, as Kay drove onto the deserted grounds, it seemed odd not to see any patients on the paths. There were few streetlights that were working along the drive and they gave off only enough light to brighten a circle in front of the entrance of each building.

As she drove, the buildings that were so drab and colorless during the day became menacing and soulless at night. They appeared suddenly out of the darkness and then faded back into the shadows. An occasional mournful cry would drift from the barred windows causing Kay to shiver and roll up her car window. The cries from the patients during the day disturbed Kay, but at night and alone, they were sad and frightening. Some of the cries were accompanied by debris thrown out the barred windows. It was as though that the sound of her passing car triggered the patients' need for attention.

She was happy to pass the Citadel, the old main building which had been a landmark for the ships sailing the sound but was in the process of being demolished. The windows of its fourteen floors now stared with vacant eyes out over the water. The knights at the corners of the top of the building were stained and green with bird droppings.

Next to the Citadel was the one story building that contained the Department of Safety. The section that housed the small fire department was closed and any calls regarding a fire went out to the local volunteer fire department. The garage that once held two fire engines and two ambulances now held one emergency vehicle and seven police cars.

She breathed a sigh of relief when she saw the cheerful lights of the small police station as she pulled into the driveway. She parked the car and went down to the basement where the offices for the security force was located.

Dane greeted her with a warm hug and a warmer kiss, "You can't possibly know how happy I am to see you."

She flushed and put the picnic basket on top of his desk, "I brought a bottle of Bolla to go with the veal."

Dane grinned with delight, he had recently started drinking wine with their meals, "Do you mind if we heat the meal right away?"

She shook her head, "I'm starved."

They put the food in the microwave and poured the wine. Kay sipped her drink and as she watched Dane move about the room setting out plates and silverware, she felt herself warming and flushed as she felt a sudden the moistness in her groin.

It was as though he sensed her arousal. He turned and reached for her and they fell onto the cot into a furious tangle of clothes and fumbling embrace. She gasped with pain at the size of his organ as he entered her. She briefly thought of Donny and his small penis and how he often ejaculated as soon as he mounted her.

She was moist, so that the initial pain quickly subsided as fire swept from her vagina to her breasts. As the heat grew, she murmured incoherently and began to thrust upward to meet his plunges. When she came the first time, she sobbed as her body shuddered, her hands grasped his buttocks trying to bring him further into her. Dane kept plunging and she felt the heat rising again, her face flushed and with a look of pain. She screamed "Never" as orgasm after orgasm shook her as he groaned loudly and rocked above her. Never had she experienced the nerves in her body being as alive as they were now.

They lay spent, beads of perspiration coating her upper lip as she lay back with one arm over her breasts and the other covering her eyes. Neither she nor Dane were aware of the burning eyes that peered out at them from the hole above the filing cabinets.

As they turned to each other in another embrace, they were startled by screaming that sounded like that of the howling of an animal in pain. It gradually receded away from them and they attributed it to the strong offshore wind blowing in from the sound.

➤ Chapter 12

Drack fled the scene at the police station, his mind flashing back and forth of memories of the Teehan slut, naked and in the arms of the cop. His temples felt as if they were going to burst with the emotion, remembering his mother, naked, screaming with lust, just like the Teehan slut. The night he took his mother, she was in the same position, legs in the air, mouth agape and moaning.

Drack roamed the catacombs in a killing rage, looking for a victim. Anyone. His rage enabled him to ignore Belial's orders to go back and take the slut and her lover. It was a Sunday evening, the institution was nearly empty of staff and visitors, thus he found no one in the deserted hospital hallways. Drack settled for going to his collection room and drugging himself. After fondling the mason jars and remembering the events surrounding each victim, he masturbated.

Drack finally went upstairs to pack for his trip to his lawyer's offices. In the midst of packing, he realized that he would have to make the house burglar proof. It was not unheard of that one of the patients seeking drugs or loot to pay for drugs, would break into one of the doctor's houses.

Thoughts of having someone in his home during his absence frightened him enough to drive him downstairs to look over the points of entry to his home.

The windows of all the homes on Doctors row were barred. It had been necessary ever since the advent of the transfer of violent criminals to Queens Park. Drack had also installed deadbolts and crossbars on the front and backdoors. He felt secure in the knowledge that the house was burglar proof when he was absent.

The problem was the inability to put the crossbar in place when leaving the house to go on duty.

He solved that problem by putting both crossbars in place and leaving the house by going out through the exit of his collection room into the catacombs. It was just a short walk through the catacombs to the vacant Citadel and out into the hospital grounds. Drack had expended weeks of time and effort in disguising this exit so that it would take a careful inspection to discover the door.

Drack went upstairs again and began to pack. As he was taking clothes from his dresser, he froze. Lately he had fallen into a trance and found himself minutes later in the same pose after revisiting the past. It was as though he went into a time warp in his mind.

His thoughts flickered like an out of sync movie film, bringing pictures of the past, long buried, of his childhood on the farm and its ancient buildings located in the small hamlet of Egypt.

The town and surrounding land was settled after the revolutionary war by freed English bond slaves and former Hessian prisoners of war. The biblical fervor of the people of the area was reflected by the names of the towns that sprang up around Egypt such as Jobtown and Jakobtown.

The towns and farms were located in the center of the great pines and swamplands of Central New Jersey. Its inaccessibility effectively isolated the people from modernizing influences of the nearby large cities of Trenton and Philadelphia. World War 2 brought hundreds of thousands of young men to an expanded Fort Dix for basic training, but even this diversity of people made little impression on the area. The soldiers were only at Fort Dix for six weeks of basic training and then sent on to other camps to be attached to a permanent division. The few hours of liberty the men received were spent in the brothels and bars of Wrightstown.

The war and the great postwar boom in industry and housing swirled around the Great Pines as though it was the eye of a hurricane and left the area virtually untouched. Constant intermarrying and inbreeding further developed a community with a personality and accent that was a language that was unique to the area.

Drack's family was typical of these natives with a blend of English cockneys, Hessian soldiers and the remnants of the local Indian tribes. Culture, customs and indeed, even appearances gave the people the name, The Pineys.

The buildings of Drack's family farm was constructed similar to that of their neighbors, with pine wood cleared from the land they cultivated and from the one small forest of oaks that lay on the edge of the pines.

Many of the first buildings were built without the use of metal. The hinges and hasps were carved out of wood and holes augured in them and then wooden pegs driven in to hold them fast.

One of Drack's ancestors, a Hessian officer with an excellent knowledge of carpentry, built sturdy buildings. The houses and barns were laid with thick oaken beams as supports. All the window casings and stairs leading to the second floor of the house were made of wide, hewn oak.

Using a local dowser, and finding a swiftly moving stream, he dug his well sixty feet into the earth and it supplied the farm with pure water through the severest of droughts. The well, its walls covered by rocks from the local quarry, was located at the end of the house, covered with a small shed that also served as a laundry room. The shed was connected to the main house so that there was never a need for the people of the farm to venture out into inclement weather for water.

The swiftly flowing stream fed the spring and pool that broke through to the surface in the stretch of woods adjacent to the family farm. An early settler sank stones around the area where the spring bubbled through the surface to form a permanent grotto. Through the centuries, the stream never dried up, providing water for the local farmers and their stock in the severest of droughts.

An early English settler, banished to the colonies because of his belief in the Druids, claimed the forest was inhabited by spirits. An aura of reverence and superstition was created around the woods and no one ever entered into the area except for a need for its water.

Although local hunters shunned the area, it was rare to see game of any kind in the woods. It was as though the animals sensed danger in the forest. The area was appropriately named Cold Spring Woods.

The memory of the burning smithy at the bottom of the lane leading to the family farm and the trapped people in the flames, screaming in agony until the collapsing roof and walls silenced them, snapped his mind back to the present.

Kay and Dane became constant lovers, stealing every moment they could to be together. It was as though the years were rolled back and they were teenagers again. They held hands when walking and kissed passionately when greeting each other. Their friends smiled knowingly and were happy for them.

They set up light housekeeping in Dane's office and brought utensils in so that they could prepare lunches during the week. Dane replaced the cot with a convertible couch, when opened up, made a comfortable bed.

Their lovemaking became more and more passionate as they discovered each others erogenous zones. Kay's arousal time became shorter but she still felt pain when he first entered her. Dane suggested that she orally moisten him but she refused, feeling that she wasn't ready for that type of sex as yet. She solved her dilemma one day by bring a vaginal cream to the station. When he became hard, she put some cream in her hands and massaged his penis. His reaction was electric, his head twisted from side to side and he groaned with passion. She too became aroused to a fever pitch and when he lifted her onto his shaft, she came several times almost instantly and without pain.

It was not unusual for them to meet at their tryst on lunch hour. Kay would appear back at her desk, her face with the unmistakable flush from sexual exertion. Donna was quick to notice and laughingly commented on how well she looked. They still continued to avoid making love in either of their houses.

Dane kept wooing Kay's children by taking them on surprise trips and attending their sporting events. The youngest girl was an excellent gymnast and she was thrilled to learn that Dane excelled in the sport as a youth. Eddie played football for his high school and Dane attended his games when he could. The boy ignored his presence and Dane gradually stopped attending.

It stung Dane occasionally, when he thought of his own two girls and that he should be spending such time with them. He thrust such thoughts at out of his mind as quickly as they entered.

Kay's sister and her husband were happy and supportive of Kay and her new romance. They offered to mind Kay's children should they decide to take a weekend trip away. Neither Kay or Dane felt secure enough in their relationship as yet to take them up on their offer.

Meanwhile Nugent and Donna were openly dating and Donna made no secret that she and Nugent had also embarked on an affair. The policeman was already moving belongings into her house.

⇒ Chapter 13

Drack guided the car from the crowded Long Island Expressway and onto the Bronx Whitestone Bridge and then into that appalling stretch of highway, the Cross Bronx Expressway. He crossed the George Washington Bridge into New Jersey and was moving west along Route 80, when his mind was captured by the boredom of the drive.

Drack remembered the unending drudgery of labor he endured as a child. He would be shaken awake while it was still dark and stumbled down to the lower pasture to drive the cows up for the morning milking. He and his sister would milk the seven cows into the silver pails and carry them two at a time to the kitchen where his mother had the big metal milk cans that were dropped off by the milk company. The milk was poured through thick cheesecloth and the heavy cream was put aside to be churned later for butter. While his sister did the churning, he scurried off to feed the pigs, chickens and horses. His sister would then join him in gathering the eggs from the nests in the filthy hen houses.

The eggs were put aside so that when they were through their chores after school, they would candle them one by one, putting each egg up to a hole cut in a cigar box with a strong light in back of it. When a fertile egg was found, it was put aside for hatching. He smiled remembering when one of the chicks was born with only one leg. He was fascinated watching the older chickens pecking at it until it died.

If there was time after a hasty breakfast, they would try to wash the farm odor from their bodies before running for school.

The one time that he ever had money in his pocket was the season he picked blueberries in the bogs just outside the Pines. The excitement of being picked up at the collection point and riding in the back of the flatbed truck with other local children was a rare treat. He would be given an apron and was taught to tie it around his waist and place two pint baskets into the apron and go down a row of the tall blueberry bushes. The berries were unlike the small wild blueberries on his farm but were hanging in clusters like grapes, easy to pick. When the baskets were full, he would go to the end of the row and wait for one of the straw bosses to come and punch his ticket indicating how many baskets he picked. At the end of the day, he would line up with the other pickers, mostly migrant workers, and present his ticket for payment. He was staggered at the amount he received, eleven dollars in cash. His excitement was short-lived. As soon as he arrived home, his chores were waiting. His mother held out her hand and took the money from him.

He was allowed to bring home two quarts of the blueberries each day from the bogs. These his mother canned at the end of the week. Drack was fascinated by the process and the experience stood him in good stead later in life.

He arrived at the lawyers offices in Bordentown and didn't remember driving the last thirty miles.

Brendan Ryan was driving the tractor with a huge mower attached to the rear, in the fields adjacent to the woods. The trees served as a buffer between the high school and the hospital. The recent heavy rainfall accelerated a late growth of grass and weeds throughout the hospital grounds, causing a last mowing that was to be done on the grounds before next spring. The sudden downpour cut small gullies in the ground causing Brendan to maneuver the mower in wide turns. His protective ear covers effectively shut out the grinding noise of the mower and it was a flock of late arriving ducks fluttering to the pond at his right that caught his attention. It was then that he noticed the two dogs tugging at what appeared to be a tree limb from the side of a gully. He stopped the tractor and squinted at the object and recoiled in sudden horror. It was a leg, the cloth surrounding it in tatters.

Brendan jumped from the tractor and ran to the site and gagged as he realized that the remains of a body were clearly visible in the exposed earth. He attempted fruitlessly to chase the dogs away and then ran for the hospital's police station at the edge of the field.

Dane looked up from his stack of paperwork as the red-faced, perspiring Brendan pounded into the building rasping, "There's a body in the woods down by the water. It's in pieces."

Dane was momentarily shocked into inactivity at the bizarre words that didn't fit in with the quiet fall day, "Who is it?"

"Jesus, Mary and Joseph! I didn't look any further than an arm and a leg."

Dane drove across the meadow past the idling tractor to where the two dogs were still tugging at something in the ground. It was the torso of a woman with gaping holes where her breasts and vagina had been. Her body was split open from the chest to her groin. The stench hit him a blow in the stomach, causing a roiling that threatened to bring up his lunch.

He motioned for Brendan to stay back. The two dogs had retreated a few yards away and were standing, tongues hanging, watching him. Dane was careful not to disturb anything in the grave, calling over his shoulder and tossing his car keys to Brendan, "Drive back to my office and call 911. Tell them it's a homicide."

Dane didn't turn around as the car left racing towards his office. He squatted over the shallow grave and with a small branch, carefully brushed away earth from the top of the corpse. He winced at the terrible wounds in the area where her breasts should have been. The corpse was a female and the killer had made terrible slashing wounds to her chest and genitals. He carefully brushed away the last remaining grains of earth from her face and blonde hair.

The first to arrive were two young Suffolk troopers who after seeing the condition of the remains backed away from the grave bringing Dane with them. While one was questioning he and Brendan, the other brought out stakes and a wide yellow plastic ribbon from the trunk of their car and began cordoning off a large area around the grave. As Dane was identifying himself, a second patrol car rolled up and Pat Nugent got out on the passenger side and wordlessly shook hands with Dane as he viewed the body in the grave. The young trooper finished his interrogation of Dane and walked over to help the other trooper cordon off the graves.

A few curious onlookers, mostly patients, gathered quickly behind the yellow tape.

Nugent grabbed Dane's arm and walked him back to the patrol car, "You're as white as a ghost. I'd have thought you'd be used to scenes like this."

Dane shook his head, "I've seen gunshot wounds and stabbing victims in the city but none as bad as this."

"Homicide and forensics should be here shortly, let's go back to your office and get a cup of coffee while we're waiting."

As they drove back to Danes office, Nugent asked, "Any idea who she is?"

Dane shook his head, "She's pretty badly disfigured.

"Fingerprints or DNA will tell us who she is."

They had just taken their first sips of coffee, when one of the troopers drove up and ran into the building, "Sarge. You'd better get back down there. We just found another body."

When Dane and Nugent arrived back at the site, a second body had been uncovered next to the first grave. Nugent and Dane crouched over the site. The body hadn't been in the ground as long as the first corpse but was disfigured in the same fashion. Dane saw a gold bracelet around the girls ankle and with a stick moved it around so they could read the inscription. They had found the missing O'Hara girl.

⇒ Chapter 14

Drack finished signing the papers naming him the sole heir to the estate. There was little in actual cash assets. The legal fees for his uncles trial, the inheritance tax and the current lawyers fees for settling the estate ate up most of the money. There was however, over two hundred acres of prime farmland, comprised of his uncle and his parents' farms. At current market value, he was a wealthy man.

He drove the few miles from the lawyers offices in Bordentown, through the small towns of the pines. As he navigated the narrow blacktop highway, it was as though he was traveling back in time. The area remained unchanged through all the years. He passed through the small towns with the same few dwellings in each, mostly gas station and general store combinations.

His car was alone on the road for the entire trip into Egypt. The only sign of life he passed was a lonely farmer turning the earth over for the next spring planting or an occasional small herd of milk cows drifting towards a far off barn for the evening milking.

Before he entered the small town of Egypt, he paused briefly, at the dirt road leading into Cold Spring woods, remembering.

After driving another mile, he pulled his car onto a grassy patch at the side of the highway and the pile of rubble that was the old smithy.

From where he was parked he had a clear view up the lane that was the access to his parents house. The driveway was now blacktopped and small pines were planted along the sides making the approach attractive on the way to the farmhouse.

He ignored the curious eyes he knew were watching him from McCrory's general store across the highway.

His father left the farm one night and never returned. He was gone for two years when his mother first joined the coven. Until then, he and his sister worked long hours in the fields and the beatings were regular and intense. His only escape from the cruelty was the small library that the county set up in the back of the general store. He escaped from his miserable existence into the novels of Zane Grey and Rafael Sabatini.

The roly-poly wife of the owner of the general store was delighted in acquiring such an avid reader since it increased the turnover in her small store of books and enabled her to keep receiving the fifteen dollars a month she was paid for maintaining the library. Soon she was allowing him to select the following months supply of books that the county would ship in to her.

He read voraciously whatever he would find in the small library and it enabled him to learn faster in all subjects at the local three room grammar school where his only intellectual competition were the farmers' sons who were only marking time until their sixteenth birthday when they could quit school and earn a man's wages.

His mother was sardonic and cruel to the excellent marks he received and the beatings were intensified. They ceased suddenly when a few months later she had brought he and his twin sister to their first black mass. It was also at the time he discovered Byron and a small book on De Sade that changed his reading tastes.

At one of the masses, one of the celebrants was a stranger whose bearded face and form was continually in shadow and always seemed to be out of focus.

After the first night, his sister became the favorite partner of his uncle and became impregnated at one of these orgies. A baby was born in pain and secrecy at the farm.

A month later, he and his twin were present and shared in the frenzied and cannibalistic sacrifice of the child. It was hung over the gourd with the goat's horns and one of the celebrants slit it's throat. The blood was drunk and the remains eaten by the coven. His sister retreated into a deranged and silent world of her own.

One night, soon after the sacrifice, their mother left the woods early, with the two children, her brother and the stranger with the goatee. Upon reaching home, she immediately chased them to their upstairs bedroom.

Soon, noises from the parlor caused the boy to creep cautiously down the wide oak stairs to the kitchen below. He pushed the kitchen door ajar. The three were entwined as one, groaning and thrashing. His mother, her blonde hair flailing with exertion and legs thrust straight up in the shape of a V, in the middle.

A red film descended over his eyes and through it came flashbacks of wild scenes in the woods. He observed himself, as if he was another person, pick up the huge knife used to prepare chickens and advance towards the semi-conscious people. He paused momentarily over his comatose mother and then suddenly brought the knife down in a series of thrusts. He whirled around at the gasp from the open door.

His twin stood there, a shadowy figure, hand to mouth and starting to scream. In almost slow motion he sprang at the shadows to stop the screaming.

When it was over, he walked to where his uncle was laying, his eyes closed, in a drunken stupor. It didn't seem strange to him to note that the red faced stranger was no longer present. Carefully he smeared his uncles hand with blood and placed the knife in it and closed his fingers around the hasp. Then he ran to the town constable's house to report the murders.

The man was actually a part time constable appointed by the county sheriff. His real profession as the caretaker and grave digger for the town's cemetery gave him little preparation for the tale of horror the boy unfolded. He asked few questions as the boy filled him in on the occurrences in the woods and finally the murders at the farm.

When he spoke of he and his sister being forced to participate in the orgies in the woods, the constable's wife threw a shawl around her shoulders and went grimly out into the night.

It seemed only moments before she reappeared with neighbors, some armed with shotguns, others with clubs and pitchforks. Telephone calls alerted more farmers on the outskirts of the county and they soon arrived at the home of the constable.

Hard eyed, grim faced men headed for Cold Spring Woods, stopping only to march up to the farm and come back with his uncle, screaming obscenities and thrashing against his bonds.

As the posse rounded the bottom of the lane and started up the highway for the woods, they ran into two carloads of the coven heading for their homes. A fight ensued and when shots were fired, the coven sought the shelter of the abandoned smithy. The constable and his men milled around the smithy demanding the people to come out and surrender or to at least release the children.

Suddenly, an intense fire broke out at the only exits from the smithy. The blaze spread rapidly to the old wooden walls and shingled roof. The screaming of those trapped inside ceased only when the walls and roof had crashed with a burning crescendo of sparks and flames shooting upward into the dark night.

His uncle was taken to the county seat, tried for murder and declared hopelessly insane and committed for the rest of his life into the state asylum at Rahway.

Drack was sent to a foster home on a farm in the next county. A couple named Robinson who specialized in boarding orphans of the county, took him in to help in working their huge farm. They fed him well and didn't cheat on the clothing allowance the county provided. He went with them and their slow witted son to the small wooden church in Jobtown every Sunday night for the three hour service. To his amazement, he had the rest of Sunday free to himself. He found another local library in the parlor of a widow three miles from the farm and would walk there early on a Sunday and fill up on books.

The Robinson boy worshipped him and followed him everywhere. They trapped a woodchuck up a tree and using the Robinson boy's air rifle kept shooting at it until it fell from its perch. Using their hunting knives, they cut open the animal while it was still alive. Neither boy showed any feeling as the animal writhed and snapped until it died from its wounds.

During the planting, growing and reaping seasons, he worked from false dawn to just past dark in the fields and barns of the farm. The off season he spent at the elementary school, with its semesters regulated around the farmers seasons. The school started on the first of October, just past reaping and finished in March just before sowing. To make up for lost time there were no school holidays excepting for Christmas.

The couple scrupulously obeyed the laws and sent him to the nearby high school, where he surprised everyone by rapidly becoming an honor student. His lack of interest in sports and the opposite sex isolated him from the rest of the student body with no friends either in school or on the neighboring farms.

Drack graduated from high school, far and away the best in his class and with scholarship offers from several colleges.

The night of his graduation he went to his parents' farm and dug in the earth between the two giant oaks that stood sentinel in front of the house. He had to go two or three feet into the firm earth before he came upon the metal box he knew was buried there. It contained all the money his family accumulated over the years. His parents, not trusting banks, simply buried what money they didn't need.

Drack fled the area that night and caught a Greyhound bus from Bordentown for New York City without regrets.

Dane and Nugent were still talking when a slender man with thinning black hair and cold blue eyes came in. Nugent rose, smiling as he shook his hand, "Dane say hello to Bill Dicks. Bill is with homicide at Suffolk County Headquarters. This is Jim Dane. He heads the security force on the grounds. Jim was a sergeant on the job in New York until he retired."

Dicks shook hands and slumped wearily into a chair gratefully accepting the coffee Dane offered to him, "Thanks. I was up most of the night on a case. I had just gotten to sleep when they woke me up at home to answer this call." Seeing the look of surprise on Dane's face, "Homicide is headquartered in Yaphank. It doesn't make sense for us to report in there every day and then go out on calls. We're supplied with cars and radios. Sometimes it works out for me and sometimes for the county."

Dane said, "It's got to be tough on your family."

Dicks nodded and held his cup out for a refill, "I've just been down at the site. One of the forensic people thinks the women have been killed within the last three months. We'll know more when the rest of our forensic team gets here. They were killed in the same way with multiple stab wounds and mutilation of the sexual organs." He shook his head trying to erase the scene from his mind, "For starters, do you have a missing persons list that we could use?"

Dane looked unhappy, "No. It shocked me when I first took over this job, how lax they are in tracking their patients who escape. I know that the second body was a missing patient of ours. Are you that certain that the other victim was a patient here?"

The detective nodded, "There aren't any locals missing and this seems to be a logical place to start. How many have escaped or declared missing since you've been here?"

"It ranges from thirty to forty. It's difficult to assess accurately since some of the patients are voluntary and simply walk off the grounds without signing out. The only ones we report missing are the patients who have been committed here by the courts. You must have noticed that there is no security on these grounds. People who are given treatment passes walk the grounds at will. Most of those who wander off the grounds will pop up in town and one of the local merchants will get pissed off and call us to come get them. We call you guys and you bring them back to us."

"What happens then?"

Dane shrugged, "They take away their treatment pass for a month or so, which restricts them to their building and any of their classes or projects they're attending. Other than that, there's nothing else we can do."

Dicks said, "I'm surprised that you don't have staff accompanying them when they're walking the grounds."

"They try to but with the constant down sizing of the staff, there aren't enough people to do the job. The governor, in an attempt to balance his budget, is closing down this facility in a few years. When people retire or quit they aren't being replaced."

Dicks looked interested, "Where do the patients go from here when it closes?"

Dane shrugged, "The criminally violent ones will be sent to other hospitals. Some will be put into halfway houses. Most of them will be dumped onto the streets."

Dicks was startled, "That's a hell of a note. We have enough crazies on the street now."

"It's going on all over the country. Who's going to go to bat for them?"

They were quiet for a moment, Dane continued, "I'm pretty sure that one of the victims is a recent escapee, Mary O'Hara."

Dane was surprised at Dicks reaction, "God damn it! I thought so. I saw the ankle bracelet too. I was afraid of this. Now the shit will really hit the fan."

Dane looked inquiringly at the detective. It was Nugent that explained, "The O'Hara kid was the niece of a connected family. Her aunt is the likely candidate to run against the governor next fall. When she was told the kid was gone, she insisted on detectives being assigned to the case. Billy here was one of them, despite it being a missing person and not a homicide. That is until now. When the media gets hold of this, it'll be a circus."

Dicks said gloomily, "The first reporters had shown up as I was coming here. I left my partner to do the talking to them."

Dane hesitated, "I don't want to intrude on your turf but have you considered that if we have two buried there, we could have more?"

Dicks eyes glinted, "Very astute, Jim. That's why it's so important that we trace every person missing for the last year. I'm pretty sure we have a serial killer on our hands and judging by the two bodies buried in the same location, we have a territorial killer. There is a strong possibility that there could be more buried around here."

Ignoring Nugent's, "Jesus Christ", Dane said, "You sound like an authority on the subject."

Dicks shook his head, "Not really. When we had that nut running around killing those prostitutes, I was selected to attend one of the FBI's regional training schools on the subject. Two weeks sure didn't make me an expert, but I have some material I brought back from the seminar. I'll start reviewing them tonight." He sighed as he arose, "I'd better get back to the site and face those reporters. I would appreciate your getting me a list of people as soon as you can that are missing for the last year."

Dane watched the two policemen leave and realized that Kay would have access to a missing persons list through the database on the computer. He reached for the phone.

Chapter 15

Drack listed the property with a realtor in Bordentown who specialized in the marketing of farmland. The agent assured him that the property would go for top dollar from either a giant farm combine or a land developer. As he drove back to Queens Park, he was jubilant at the size of his inheritance.

Drack planned to take the money and an early retirement from the hospital. The combination of funds would allow him to lead a comfortable existence. He was smiling as he played his tapes of Wagner all the way home. He played over and over, his favorite, the martial, drumming, and exciting, Dies Valkyrie.

His euphoria was short lived. When he approached the toll booths at the Bronx Whitestone Bridge, he bought a Newsday from one of the newsboys. He glance at the front page as he waited on line at the toll booth and halted the car in shock. The front page of the paper was in bold black print. Two bodies were found on Queens Park grounds and the reporter quoted an unnamed source that there was speculation that these might not be the complete count.

Drack pulled over to the side at the first rest stop he came to and read the article. The reporter claimed that sources in the police department said that the close location of the victims graves might indicate that a serial killer was on the loose in the area of the hospital. A picture of the O'Hara girl in her cheerleading uniform was next to a photo of an attractive grey haired woman, identified as the girl's aunt. The woman, a prominent politician was quoted as demanding an independent investigation of conditions at the hospital.

A specially trained team of police dogs were going to be brought to the grounds of the hospital to see if any more bodies were present.

Alarmed and fearful, Drack drove the remainder of his trip to his house haunted by his thoughts and unable to plan ahead. As he came closer to Queens Park, the whispers from Belial became stronger and more violent.

Dane sat on the edge of the bed holding the picture of Anna and the girls in his hands. Sighing, he put it back on his nightstand and padded barefoot to the kitchen. As he waited for the coffee to perk, he gazed out the window, remembering how happy they were when they moved into the secluded North Shore town of Dix Hills.

He came out of his reverie as the coffee gurgled its announcement that it was through perking. As he finished his breakfast, he moodily contemplated the morning's news conference at the hospital. The discovery of the bodies on the grounds of the hospital made headlines in the papers in the metropolitan area. Camera crews were set up at all the entrances to the hospital. The local police were effective in keeping them from entering the grounds but found it impossible to keep individual reporters from walking onto the grounds and interviewing anybody they wished.

The narrow roads leading to the hospital was jammed with spectators. The police solved the problem by setting up roadblocks at all the access roads and allowing only hospital personnel to enter. The hospital workers were ordered to wear their passes around their necks for easy identification.

Dr, Liebman was excited at first and gave pompous interviews to journalists and television reporters at every opportunity. His comments on the case angered the police and it wasn't until he received a call from Albany that his fifteen minutes of fame was deflated. Under strict orders from Albany, he was to avoid any comments on the case and to forward questions from the press to the police in charge of the investigation. Any questions regarding hospital security was to be handled by the head of security. A press conference was to be held each day at the front of Options house which was located at the front entrance. Any reporter violating this order was to be picked up by the hospital security and turned over to the local police for prosecution. The health of the patients was to be cited as the main reason for the tightening of security.

A subdued Dr. Liebman ordered Dane to represent the hospital security and asked Dicks to attend the press conference.

The porch of Options house was set up with microphones and used as a forum for the press conference. Dr. Liebman introduced Dicks and Dane to the reporters and stepped back. As he was talking, Dicks whispered to Jack, "Damn, that woman in the front row on the left is the O'Hara girl's aunt. This is going to be a circus."

As he spoke, one of O'Hara's aides brought her a chair. The movement caught the eyes of one of the television crews and it swung its camera towards her.

The first question was the usual one in all murder cases, "Lieutenant Dicks, do you have any suspects?"

"No. We are just now identifying the remains of those we've found so far."

One of the older reporters picked up on the statement. "Are you saying that there may be more bodies?"

Dicks held up his hands, "Guys. I mean that we don't know anything specific to really answer questions such as this."

A torrent of inane questions were thrown at Dicks and he parried them as best he could with growing impatience. The same reporter who picked up on Dick's reference to other bodies had been looking hard at Dane, "Mr. Dane, I believe I met you while you were working for the New York City Police. I'm sure that you were one of the lead detectives on a serial killer case in Manhattan. Is that correct?"

"Yes I was on the force until I retired and came out here to the hospital."

"Wasn't that also a serial killer case and wasn't it called the fruit killer case?"

Dane was surprised that the reporter called the case by the name the police gave the grisly case. It had been decided to keep the fruit angle secret.

A detective gave the killings the name because the killer placed a piece of fruit in the vagina of his victim. Headquarters at Centre Street put a veil of secrecy as to any clues regarding the case, particularly about the fruit.

"Yes. I worked on that case several years before I retired. The killer was never found and the case is still open on the books."

The aunt stood up, "May I ask a question?"

Dicks muttered to Dane "Here it comes." Loudly, "Of course Mrs. O'Hara."

"My only complaint with this hospital is its lack of security. I can't understand how a murderer could escape from a locked ward to commit these murders at night and if they were done during the day, how they could be committed under the eyes of thirty policemen.

However, the ultimate guilty party who aided in the murder of my niece is the governor of this state."

Angrily, Dane answered the woman, "You make it sound as though I had a battalion of Marines here. Most of these people are not much better than rent-a-cops. With the most recent budget cuts, there aren't enough bodies to really secure this place. And as far as telling the media that it is a patient doing the killings, you're way out of line. We don't know that it was a patient."

Dicks nodded agreement, watching the woman carefully, "It could be anyone. The grounds are wide open for anyone to come in from the outside and commit the murders. The unused, wooded grounds could hide a gang war."

The woman held her hand to her heart, "Well, I'm going to raise hell with everybody connected to this case. Particularly to that mean spirited hypocrite in Albany. He's the real murderer."

The two policemen were silent at this but Dr. Liebman said unhappily, "Mrs. O'Hara, you can't lay all the blame on Albany. They're---"

By now all the attention was on the woman, "All I'm asking is a thorough investigation into who murdered my niece and the other woman and who is to blame for the lack of security."

Dr. Liebman called an end to the press conference and walked back into Options house with Dane and Dicks. Dicks looked back over his shoulder, "She doesn't give a shit about the murders. She just threw her hat into the ring for governor."

⇒ Chapter 16

Drack remained in his home on the grounds the entire weekend, roaming restlessly from room to room, finally settling in his storage room with its huge freezer. A heavy dose of Prozac and cocaine was able to hold his demons at bay and gave him time to think. His panic subsided, and he made his plans to leave the hospital. First, he had to find someone to be a scapegoat for the sacrifices.

It was late Monday afternoon when they met. They sat around the desk in Danes office with Dane breaking the silence. "Kay, you've been a big help in developing the list of the missing people. Lieutenant Dicks has some questions he'd like to ask you. I've had it cleared with your Chief of Service for you to spend as much time as needed to assist the police in their investigation."

Kay nodded silently, still shaken by the disclosure of the dead in the meadow.

Dicks said, "Do you have a separate list of patients who have killed in the past?"

She shook her head, "I don't have an actual list, but I'm sure we can cull them from the general population by the computer number. They're scattered in different buildings in different wards."

" You mean, that they aren't in one guarded building?"

She shook her head, "No, some of them are in our BTU, that's our behavioral treatment unit in building 8 and we have them in the intensive treatment unit in building 21. We even have them in the geriatric building ."

Dicks snorted, "Geriatric killers? When I hear the word geriatric, I immediately think of grandmother types or fragile old men." He shook his head in wonder, "You had better give me a thumbnail education on what the different wards are."

Kay earnestly watched the men as she spoke, "Most of the killers in geriatrics have been there for years." She thought for a moment, "We do have a recent admittee who is seventy three who killed a man he was passing in the street. The ones in intensive treatment are those considered chronic and supposedly can be treated medically or with psychiatry and returned to our normal wards and even given the freedom of the grounds. The behavioral treatment wards are the dangerously violent killers who will probably be there forever."

Dicks held up his hands in a stop signal, "Whoa! Do you mean that people who have killed before are walking these grounds right now?" When Kay nodded, "Then, theoretically our killer could be one of them."

Kay was troubled, "It's hardly likely. Almost all of those who have the freedom of the grounds must be accompanied to and from their destinations." She hesitated, "There are three patients who are scheduled for release this week. All three have killed and were originally judged criminally insane."

Dicks was startled, "Who the hell decided to turn them loose?"

"It's really not any single person's decision. The staff is under tremendous pressure to empty our wards. They have been judged as cured by a panel of psychiatrists and are due to be released."

"We'll have to hold up on their release until I can check out their whereabouts when the murders were committed or at least until we find the actual murderer."

Kay shook her head, "It's a done deal. Not only are their attorneys aware of the release, but they have patients rights attorneys here in the hospital that would see to it that the decision is enforced."

Dicks looked thoughtful, "I can't believe that three convicted killers are being turned loose that simply."

Dane broke in, "Tell the Lieutenant about the cannibal."

Kay said, "You must have read of the high school teacher from the city who killed and ate part of his student?"

When Dicks nodded, "Well, he's been put through intensive treatment and given the freedom of the grounds without supervision. He's even teaching in one of our programs during the day."

Dicks was incredulous, "This sounds like something out of Alice in Wonderland. How the hell can anybody work under these conditions?"

Kay said, "You can't dwell on the danger or you can't work here." Then defiantly, "It's not as bad as it sounds. There are safety measures in place. The only real danger is when we have to go on the wards, particularly the ones I mentioned. As a matter of fact, most of the other patients are really very sweet."

"Well you've given me a hell of a list of suspects."

Kay shook her head in denial, "I don't think so. None of these people are on the grounds after dark and in daylight, there are so many people walking about that one crime might go undetected. But more than one?"

He looked curiously at her, "As I said before. I'm pretty sure we have a serial killer on our hands. They are extremely territorial which means that it's a good chance that the killer comes from your inmate population."

Kay sounded angry, "You're scaring me. I can't see how you can be so positive that we have a serial killer or that anyone connected to the hospital had anything to do with the bodies that were found."

"You may be right but we can't overlook any possibility and right now the patients in this hospital are a good bet. If we do have a serial killer, chances are that he's still here, since most territorial killers are also stationary. Of the five thousand unsolved murders in this country last year, thirteen hundred of them were committed by serial killers. The first case we studied at the seminar was in France in the early 1600's. A woman killed over six hundred and fifty young women so that she could bathe in their blood."

Dane was shocked, "My God! She made Jack the Ripper look like an amateur."

Dicks nodded, "She was a rarity. Eighty five percent of the serial killers in this country are white males." He looked thoughtful and added slowly, "I don't want to add to your fears but five percent of the serial killers come from the medical profession. Ours could be a patient with a medical background." Then he added deliberately, "Or it could be one of the staff from the hospital."

There was silence in the room.

⇒ Chapter 17

Drack watched fearfully from the window of his office as the young female trooper guided her German Shepherd around the ground of the last burial. Belial was screaming in his head that he had to act and now! He had to throw suspicion on someone else at the hospital. They were sure to find other burials before long. A solution came to him and Belial chuckled in agreement at the simplicity of the idea. He would drug and use autosuggestion on one of his patients to confess to the sacrifices. He would implant the thought that he committed the crimes and even tell him where the burial grounds were. But who? It would have to be someone with a violent case history and had freedom of the grounds. It would also have to be someone with a strong drug habit and easily led by suggestion. Belial was roaring with laughter as the solution came to Drack. He had the perfect patient.

Corporal Cathy Fleck let Wolf drag her as he searched along the ground. They had been at it for hours and the first thrill had worn off. This was her and Wolf's first homicide and she was excited in the beginning. She hid her emotion, trying to act as professionally as the other trooper.

She was a strong stocky woman but the big shepherd put tremendous pressure on her shoulders and hands as he tugged on the leash. Suddenly she sensed a change in Wolf's actions. He was circling over an area, his black muzzle quivering and his body tense. She signaled to the county trooper nearby, "I think he's found something."

The trooper motioned for several of the nearby workmen to grab their shovels and he raced to her side. While the workers were digging in the spot she pointed out, Wolf ran to an area not more than eight feet away. The other dog handler joined them and his dog also began circling a spot. The two state troopers stared at one another for a minute and as the workmen uncovered the first body, Cathy said to the county cop, "I think you better get a lot more diggers. We're going to need them."

Chapter 18

Drack approached Olsen while he was sitting at one of the picnic tables outside of his halfway house. The man readily ingested the LSD that he offered him. Oddly, it took several moments for the powerful drug to take effect. Drack watched closely. It was difficult to predict what direction a given person taking the drug would go. It was an added fillip that Olsen was already mentally disturbed by his addiction to Crack and alcohol.

At first, his face took a dreamy look as though he was in a trance. Drack tried reaching him, "Richard, if you can hear me, lift your hand from the table."

Drack felt a thrill as the man lifted his hand several times from the table. "I want you to remember what you have been doing for the eight years at the hospital. Will you do that?" Again Olsen raised his hand from the wood. This time, a slight frown flashed across the dream like smile.

Drack looked quickly around. The table they were sitting at was under a huge tree and couldn't be seen by a casual onlooker from the building and there was no one in sight on the grounds. It was late afternoon and the long lines of shuffling people had entered their respective buildings for the evening meals. An occasional auto made its way along the boulevard with an employee going home.

"You remember sacrificing all those girls to Belial?"

The man looked puzzled, and slowly shook his head from side to side.

His reaction stopped Drack for a moment. He then realized that Olsen didn't recognize the name of Belial, "Belial is the son of the fallen Angel that you worshipped. He has taken the master's place here and you have been acting for him. Don't you remember?"

This time the man nodded his head, slowly at first, then with a smile, more vigorously.

Drack felt Belial leave him as he asked, "Do you recognize him?"

The man became agitated and with a fearful look shrank back on the bench.

Drack took a deep breath, and began describing the sacrifices and who they were. If Olsen was unable to remember their names, he was to be honest and tell anyone who questioned him that he either didn't know the girls names or didn't know them when he sacrificed them. Olsen calmly agreed.

"From now on, the voice you will hear is that of Belial son of the fallen angel. Do you understand?"

The man gave a peculiar series of convulsions but again shook his head in understanding. Drack began to tell Olsen where the bodies on the grounds were buried and how they were killed.

Kay, Dane and Dicks were again sitting in Danes office. Dicks requested that they hold a morning meeting every day. This would free Kay to keep up her normal duties. This morning, they were examining a computer printout containing the names of people who had escaped or disappeared from the hospital in the last two years. There were over eighteen hundred names on the list. Dane was despondent. If Dicks was correct and the three girls whose bodies were down at the morgue came from this list, it was going to be a difficult task. Dental records had already verified that one of the first bodies uncovered was that of the O'Hara girl.

Dane looked up from his printout first, "Judging from the first three bodies we found I think that we can make a start by eliminating the males from within the list. The bodies all seemed to be young, so if we can go down the column on our right and only highlight with a marker those born within the last twenty five years, then we'll put a big dent in the list."

Dicks looked at Kay, "Can we get a new printout from Data Processing for all girls under twenty five from this list?"

Kay nodded and reached for the phone at the same time that a trooper came to the door, his young face beaded with sweat and red from the exertion of running. "We've just uncovered seventeen more bodies. I don't know if the dogs are through looking or not but we've got a regular cemetery down there."

Chapter 19

Drack was calm although the hospital and the entire Island was electrified by the news of the discovery of the bodies buried on the hospital grounds. He had several meetings with Olsen and reinforced the story the man would tell at the right time. The man's ability to remember most of the names and the circumstances was remarkable since his short term memory was badly disrupted by the attack the drugs and alcohol made upon it.

Drack fed him strong doses of the LSD, being careful not to overdo the dosage. He didn't want the man doing harm to himself. Drack smiled, that is, not until Olsen told the world his story.

The group, now including the chief of service, Dr. Liebman and Tony Harris, a leading physiatrist sat around the oval table in the conference room in building 15. Dicks and his partner from the county were also at the meeting.

Dicks addressed the chief of service, "I can't believe that twenty three young girls were butchered over a period of over eight years and nobody questioned their whereabouts all that time."

Dr. Liebman looked uncomfortable, "We have a shortage of staff and eight hundred acres to control. The population of this institution ranges from eight to nine thousand at any given time." The pudgy man took a sip of water, "A voluntary patient can walk out the door of any building in the complex any time he or she wants and we won't have a record on them. Albany is constantly having us throw the easier patients out on the streets and are warehousing their violently insane here."

Dicks looked disgustedly at the man who appeared ready to weep, "Doctor Harris, can you give me a profile on what our killer might look like? Perhaps we can match up your profile with that of one of the patients."

Dane interrupted before Harris could answer, " What makes you so sure that it's a patient? It could be one of the townspeople or even one of the staff."

Harris shook his head, "I think we should go on the assumption that it's one of our violent patients and if so, it has to be a long term patient who will match the time of death of the first victim. I've already compiled a list of possible suspects, with the help of Kay, here." He paused to pass out copies of the list which was several pages long. "Based on the initial reports from your forensics team, it looks as though the first victim was buried about five years ago. The patients on this list have all been here for the right time period and could be psychologically right for these crimes. We have eliminated any of those who are too physically disabled to commit such a crime. I have also taken off the list those who have been incarcerated continuously and wouldn't have the freedom to move about to be part of the murders."

The other county detective, a man named Leonard, a large beefy man with a lion like head who moved slowly enough for the casual observer to dismiss him as dull witted. That is, unless one looked into the bright intelligent eyes, spoke for the first time, "How can you be so certain that one of these birds couldn't have figured out a way to get himself loose when the time suited him?"

Dane looked up, "Don't be so certain that it's a male. Kay's told me some hair raising tales of some of the women here who could literally bend metal chairs when they became enraged? I had a personal experience with a woman in NY who put three cops out of action."

Harris said apologetically, "You're right of course. When Lieutenant Dicks said he wanted a list of all males who fit the profile of our friend, I naturally came up with a list of men only."

Leonard said, "I wasn't here for this profile that's being mentioned. What are we talking about?"

Dane said, "Your partner has some training on serial killers and came up with some FBI papers on that subject based on their experience with them. If nobody minds, I'll read you what we've come up with." He read slowly from a typewritten sheet in front of him, "Eighty five percent of the typical serial killer is a white male. Most of the female serial killers are nurses who felt they are on a mission of mercy when they kill a patient. Some have a deep seated physiological gender hate." Dane looked up at his audience, "That should preclude any of our female patients since all of the victims are women."

Dicks said, "We are working on the assumption that all of the bodies are female. Our lab people are still working on the remains. I've asked them to check first for gender. The later victims are all young women and with genital mutilation. The ones who have been in the ground longest have deteriorated too badly to determine if they were mutilated after being killed. We will be lucky to get an approximate time of death."

Dane continued, "If, as we suspect that all of the victims are young women, then we can immediately zero in on a male serial killer. Many display a triad of symptoms such as bed-wetting, arson and cruelty to animals as children.

The single biggest thread running through all serial killers is a history of childhood abuse. There is usually a string of motives connected to physiological makeup with strong sado-sexual overtones."

Leonard shifted his bulk in his chair, "How the hell can you treat these people."

Harris said defensively, "We give them medication and psychiatric therapy. New medication is continuously coming out that is controlling mental disability. Prozac has been a tremendous aid in treating the emotionally disturbed. Another that has only been on the market for a year or two has had sensational results. It is called Clostimine. It's put thousands of schizophrenic patients out of the hospital and back to leading useful lives."

"Then why isn't it being used more extensively"

Harris looked uncomfortable, "Well, there are some side effects. Not all patients can tolerate it and it is still damnably expensive."

Dicks said gravely, "What Doctor Harris is not adding is that the medication is only effective if the patient takes it regularly. If a psychopathic killer is released as being cured, and discontinues taking his medication, all we will have is a psychopath who has killed and will kill again. As far as Prozac is concerned there are a lot of people who think that it is being over prescribed and overvalued."

Harris, annoyance beginning to show, said, "We are doing the best we can. Right now we are beginning to treat those patients who don't respond to psychotherapy and antidepressants such as Prozac with ECT."

Dane said, "That's a new one. What the hell is ECT."

Dr. Liebman answered, "ECT are the initials for electroconvulsive therapy. You laymen know it as shock therapy."

Leonard was startled, "Jesus, you mean like the treatment Jack Nicholsen got in the picture. You know, the one that turned him into a zombie.

Liebman looked helplessly at Dr. Harris who answered for him, "ECT was mishandled in the fifties and sixties by people who should have used more caution. They were giving patients ECT sometimes as much as three times a day."

Dane said, "I thought it was outlawed because of the dangers involved."

"Several states, such as New York, did ban its use but it is slowly regaining a reputation that it is useful in treating schizophrenia and mania. However most of the patients we use it on are those with severe cases of depression, again only after medication has failed."

Leonard broke in, "It looks to me that psychiatry is a guessing game as far as treating these people and when you have the medicine to control them you either won't use it or can't afford to give it to everybody."

Harris rose in anger, "We have over eight thousand patients in this institution and ninety nine percent of them are good people who wouldn't hurt a fly. Your discussions and this," throwing the FBI report on the table, "if the papers ever get hold of them, they would set mental health back fifty years. Some of these patients are old people who have nowhere to go and we're turning them out on the street because Albany is trying to cover a deficit. We have people who have Alzheimer's or have withdrawn from the world. This is their only safe haven. When they're forced out, as many are, they're killed by a society they don't understand and can't defend themselves against. We have vegetables who have been warehoused here who were butchered, legally on an operating table under the guise of that magic cure all, of the fifties, the lobotomy. When I was invited to join this panel, I thought I was going to be asked to give a portrait of a possible killer in our midst. Instead, I've heard nothing but dangerous generalizations that if published in the newspapers could set mental health back to the snake pit days."

The people at the table watched in astonishment as the doctor strode from the room and slammed the door behind him.

Dicks said, "What the hell is eating him?"

Kay said angrily, "He's a caring person. You don't see the other side of the patients we have. Most of them are very ill people who are more sinned against than sinned. If you look at this list of possible suspects, you'll see that it represents only two percent of our total patient population."

Leonard spread his hands deprecatingly, "I may have used a poor choice of words but it doesn't change the fact that there is a killer on these grounds and we only have theories that he won't go off the grounds to kill." He shook his head, "I'm sorry if I offended the good doctor, but my job is to catch a killer."

Kay said, "If you do find him and he is a patient here what will happen to him? If he is a patient he is already under lock and key."

Leonard answered her, "That's a good question. If he's caught and brought to trial, even the newest and dumbest lawyer will claim insanity as a defense."

Dicks said thoughtfully, "How the hell could you punish him? Jeffrey Dahmer killed a bunch of men and admitted eating one of his victims heart. Shawcross had sex with dozens of prostitutes and then strangled them and their juries rejected the prosecution's arguments and determined that they were not guilty by reason of insanity. The serial killers almost always use the insanity plea, jurors will simply not allow a death penalty when you have crimes such as this." He shrugged, "and in this case, if it is a patient, he'll probably just get closer surveillance."

Later as Kay and Dane were leaving the conference together, Dane said, "Leonard and Dicks are cops. They don't look at your patients the same way you do. To them, everything is in black and white. The people populating this place are here because they are mentally ill. Whoever is doing these killings is obviously deranged. Ergo, they are all suspects."

"You were a policeman for many years and you don't think the same as them."

Dane's mind flashed back to his days of violent behavior under the influence of alcohol and didn't answer.

➤ Chapter 20

Drack felt the bile rise in his throat as he passed the conference room where the police and the Teehan woman were just leaving their morning meeting. His chest constricted with fear and hatred of the hospital policeman and his woman. He heard enough of the group's conversation as they stood outside the room to give him the feeling that they were closing in. He had to make his move. And now!

That night, Drack rode the ancient elevator up to the third floor to the violent ward. He didn't speak to the beefy aides sitting at the desk guarding the locked door. They lowered their magazines long enough to give him a cursory look without asking him to sign the pass book that sits outside all the wards.

He nodded slightly and entered the ward. It was just after ten o' clock and most of the patients were already asleep, under heavy sedation. He walked to the bed where Olsen lay sleeping. He hesitated, trying to remember exactly how he used thought control the last time.

He experimented on a troublesome patient and led him to the roof of one of the buildings in the middle of a severe Northeaster that dropped sixteen inches of snow on Long Island. Drack left the man sitting against one of the ducts and told him to stay there until he returned for him.

They found the patient when the snow melted, five days later sitting in the same position that Drack left him.

As he started to bend over Olsen, a scene flashed before him. He was in the clearing in Cold Spring Woods watching a man dressed as Satan coupling with a young girl. Her face was hidden in shadow but her slim body, blonde hair fanned out on the ground, writhing and contorted was clear in the light of the dancing flames of the fire.

As quickly as the scene appeared, it vanished, leaving him shaken and still bent over Olsen. These flashes were occurring more frequently now. He would find himself standing as though in a trance when he came out from one of the scenes. His mind had become a house of memories and when he came out of a blackout, a wall of the house collapsed leaving more of the interior of the room open to view.

At the insistent urging of Belial, he began whispering in Olsen's ear.

They drove into the city early on a Sunday, with Dane and Kay doing all the talking. The children had made plans of their own with friends and didn't want to go on the day trip. They settled into a resentful silence and only spoke in response to a direct question. Eddie, the oldest was particularly hostile, while Kim, his sister finally took an interest in the trip. Dane and Kay had discussed the children's continued antipathy towards him. The only answer seemed to be further day excursions in an effort to have them warm up to him.

Dane parked his car in front of Trinity Church located at the foot of Wall Street. He was surprised to see barricades up to prevent automobile traffic from entering the famous street. One of the policemen on duty told him that the barricades were up to prevent terrorist attacks on the financial institutions.

The heavy tourist trade had not begun its onslaught as yet and parking was plentiful. They visited the historic graves in the graveyard of the historic old church. Kim in particular was a history buff and was fascinated by the famous names on the gravestones that she read in her history books.

When they left the church, Dane intended to drive around the historic financial section but because of the barricades took them on a walking tour instead. He pointed out the headquarters of the huge financial institutions located on Wall Street and the narrow winding streets that abutted the area. During the walk, Kim opened up and asked questions.

It was while they were having lunch that Dane made his first real breakthrough to Eddie. They were eating in a restaurant at the foot of Beaver Street where it ended at Hanover Square. It was owned by a friend he had known when he was a beat cop in downtown Brooklyn.

They had just sat down ordered drinks, and were looking at the menu when the owner, Mike Marino, came in. Spotting Dane, he immediately came over and effusively hugged him and chatted briefly to Kay and the children. He apologized for having to leave so soon but was due uptown for a meeting in another one of his restaurants. Before Marino left, he instructed the waiter in front of the group that Dane's party were the guests of the house.

Kay noticed the interest in the children's eyes at the respect the man paid to Dane and said, "Where do you know him from?"

"Mike owned a small Italian bar and restaurant that was on my beat in Brooklyn Heights. I usually stopped in for a drink with him after my tour. One night I walked in on a holdup. There were three of them and they caught Mike tallying up the weekend receipts. I broke it up."

Kim, with wide eyes, "Was anybody hurt?"

"There were only a couple of shots fired. They were just kids and had started drinking Mike's whiskey and couldn't have hit a barn door. One of the kids was slightly wounded and the others dropped their guns when they saw blood. Mike was sure that they were going to kill him and his help. One of the waiters knew one of the kids and they were talking about not leaving any witnesses. Anyway, Mike has really done well since then. He opened this spot and has moved uptown with three more. He's going to open a real fancy one in the Hamptons next spring and I have an invitation for the grand opening. If you like, you can join me as my guests."

The children eyed Dane with respect were thrilled with the invitation. The rest of the day was spent in the South Seaport as an animated group and they finished up with an excellent dinner before heading back out to the Island.

Kay whispered to Dane by the car as he was going home, "I think everything is going to be fine."

The next morning when Dane was laying out the shifts for the men for that week, a nurse phoned him, "Jim, you had better get up to Building 15. One of the patients has killed a girl and is sitting out front in the parking circle by the body."

Dane reached into his desk and brought out the revolver that was a memento from his days on the force. The hospital security force were not allowed to carry firearms but Dane had secured a permit from Suffolk County for his pistol. He stuffed it into a side pocket and headed towards the scene.

137

When he arrived there, he was met with a chilling sight. Olsen was sitting on the ground next to a gory, unrecognizable body of a young woman. He had a long bloody knife in his hand.

Her body was laying face up and her clothing was cut down the middle and lying open like the wrapping of a Christmas package. Her throat was slashed ear to ear and she was mutilated from her breasts to her groin. A late fall fly buzzed languorously around the blood on her throat.

Dane walked through the crowd of patients and hospital personnel and motioned to them to move back. The white jacketed attendants began forcing the people away from the scene. He said, "Put the knife down, Olsen. Nobody is going to harm you."

The man sat there motionless, streaks of black dye running through his blonde hair. His eyes were opaque and unfocussed. Dane had the eerie feeling that he was peering into the windows of an abandoned building.

The man stirred when wailing sirens announced the arrival of the county police. As their car doors slammed, he slowly arose to his feet. Dane felt rather than saw the police come up behind him. Olsen's face began contorting and he spoke rapidly and unintelligibly. The only word that came through clearly was the name, Belial. As he spoke, he started towards Dane with the knife in his hand. As he came closer, he raised the knife in a series of jerky movements.

A young trooper, eyes wide, said excitedly, "Halt! Drop the knife and lay on the ground with your hands behind your back."

Dane turned to the young trooper and said angrily, "For Christ's sake. He's on another planet. Let me handle this."

As though on an unseen command, Olsen rushed forward raising the knife and straight into a hail of bullets.

⇒ Chapter 21

Drack watched the crowd of police and spectators around the two bodies until the ambulances came and took Olsen to the hospital and the girl to the morgue. Belial and Lew laughed gleefully all the while murmuring to each other. They had recently started talking unintelligibly except when telling him to kill.

As Drack looked down at the group another tableaus passed before his eyes. It was a scene, replayed in his mind many times, of him descending into the deepest, coldest room of the old farmhouse. It was the root cellar that was dug out of the clay beneath the house. The family for generations used it to store vegetables and preserves for the winter. There were shelves along the walls lined with mason jars full of the fruits and vegetables that his mother canned. He helped in the canning and was fascinated by the preservation process. The experience was a great help when he began collecting trophies from his victims.

He watched over the shoulders of his mother and saw the girl burying the few remains of the body of a baby. The child was her second pregnancy and was stillborn at birth. It was one of the few times that his mother acceded to the wishes of either of the children. The girl did not want the remains buried in Cold Spring woods as her mother wished.

He tried to clear away the haze surrounding the girl's face. As she turned to face the lantern he held, the face was that of his sister. The haze began to lift and the scene would fade from his mind.

The sudden look into the past and quick departure always left Drack trembling and drenched in perspiration. The last incident left him with a weakness in his left side and a slight limp.

Olsen was rushed to St. Marks hospital, grievously wounded but still alive. The man made a rambling deathbed confession telling Dicks and the team of homicide detectives where some of the bodies were buried. The detectives were puzzled as to his vagueness to some of the questions they asked. Later, they attributed it to his pain and the drugs he was being given. The angry doctor in charge kept urging them to be brief. After two days Olsen died, murmuring the name Belial.

The media, as usual created a circus-like atmosphere around the hospital. Pictures were taken of the burial sites with hospital employees pointing to the ground where a body was found. One enterprising TV camera crew went so far as to get two of the employees with shovels, supposedly digging for bodies.

Dr. Liebman was in his glory, giving out statements that were inaccurate and sometimes, hilarious. Albany sent down a gag order to the hospital and gradually the hospital returned to normalcy.

––––––––––––––––

Kay sat holding the coffee cup between her hands seeking warmth from the heat. She was afraid that if she relaxed her grip, the cup would slip to the floor and her composure with it.

Donna turned from the window, "Well, they caught the killer, thank God. It's a shame he killed again before they stopped him."

"Did they identify the girl?"

Donna nodded, "It was the Caples girl." At Kay's questioning look, she explained, "She was a retarded girl, a recurring patient that was transferred here again two weeks ago. She was referred by a Mobile Crisis teams from one of the residency houses because she was having periods of violence."

"She was retarded?"

Dr. Abbot entered the office and answered Kay's question, "She was one of my team's patients for several years. We put her on Moban and Lithium and she went from heavy sheet restraint in a week to going out on day passes."

Donna looked out the window and said, "Here comes your lover boy. He should have more info. He's got that homely detective in tow."

They were quiet as they heard Dane and Dicks mount the short flight of steps and enter Kay's office. Dane leaned down and kissed Kay, "What a day. I've spent most of it going over identification of the victims. The police are satisfied that Olsen was the killer of the rest of the victims."

Kay said, "Are you sure that he acted alone?"

Dicks nodded, "Most serial killers are loners. There has been a few exceptions like the cousins out in California. Criminals, whether they be bank robbers or killers like our boy, Olsen, have big mouths. They talk their way into trouble. In the case of serial killers, some of them will write to the press or the police, bragging about their deeds."

Abbott interjected, "I still can't believe that Olsen was a killer. He was psychotic not a psychopath."

Dane looked at Abbott, "What's the difference."

"A psychotic will withdraw from reality while a psychopath will be hostile and antisocial."

"That sounds like Olsen to me."

Abbott shook his head, "A psychotic will imagine he sees the devil, pitchfork and all. A psychopath will try to kill you with the pitchfork."

Donna shuddered, "He admitted doing the murders."

Turning to Dane, she asked, "How could they have identified the bodies so quickly. Some of them were in pretty poor shape."

"The latest ones were easy. We were able to get most of them by way of fingerprints and dental records. Thanks to Kay and the list she dug up for us, we were able to match most of them. The tough ones were the ones that were buried the longest and had deteriorated to the point that they were skeletal."

Kay was curious, "How do they identify a skeleton? Not all of our patients come in with dental records."

Dicks nodded his thanks to Dane as he was handed a cup of coffee, "They're the toughies. The forensic people took the easy ones first and identified the ones with flesh on their hands. They simply cut off the fingers and put them into alcohol solution to harden the pads and then fingerprint them." He stopped in consternation as Kay rose from her chair ashen faced, "Jesus, am I an idiot. I got so caught up in this case that I forgot where I was."

Dick got up, "I've got a meeting with forensics. God, I hope we can wrap this up by the weekend."

Donna arose, "I have to go too." She paused at the door, "Are you going to the Old Pier tonight? I'm going to meet some of the gang for a drink to celebrate the end of this horror."

Kay nodded and Donna cheerfully waved and as she and Abbott left together. Kay broke the silence, "Are they sure he committed all those murders?"

Dane was horrified, "My God! Do you think we have more than one serial killer roaming the grounds?" He shook his head, "The odds are a million to one. He did them alright, even though it will be impossible to match all his free time to the murders. The staff at the halfway house said he was a real loner and would take off on his own for hours at a time. He was also on that fringe of that Satanic cult that killed that kid last year. Besides, he gave us enough data that only the killer would know. It was him alright."

Dicks nodded assent, "It had to be him. Nothing else makes any sense." He finished his coffee, "I've got to join Abbott at that forensic meeting."

Kay watched him leave and shuddered, "We recently had a team meeting and Olsen was one of the patients we discussed. I could swear that it was recommended that he be kept under strict observation. One of the aids who was standing close to him just before he was shot, told me he heard Olsen mutter that he was told to say he killed the girls."

Dane nodded, looking troubled, "I heard him say the same thing and used the name Belial several times."

"I never heard of anybody with that name on the hospital for either staff or patient."

"Maybe you could have someone in Personnel check the name."

She nodded, "I'm sure we don't have a patient by that name, but I can do a quick scan with the computer."

As he watched, she accessed the patient list and quickly scrolled down to the B section. She looked up and shook her head.

"I wish the troopers hadn't been so quick to shoot. I could have sworn he was going to surrender." He sighed, "We'll never know"

"Do you have any idea as to when they're going to release the girls body?"

"It shouldn't be long. Why."

Kay arose from her desk and began covering her computer, "We've been trying to locate any relatives that might claim the Caples girl but apparently she's an orphan. She was committed here first when she was six. This and the other institutions were the only homes she ever knew and she considered the staff her family."

"What happens if nobody claims her?"

"We'll bury her in the cemetery on the grounds."

Dane was startled, "Jesus. I've passed that cemetery a hundred times and never gave it a thought. So that's where the unclaimed patients are buried."

Kay nodded, "It's sad. We're supposed to be the most advanced civilization in the world, but we just throw these people away. You'd be surprised at how many of the staff attend the services. Most of the staff and patients have a close relationship."

They left the building arm in arm, looking forward to an evening of relaxation. As they left, the big black patient, Minney, was busy sweeping the steps. A garish red wig was atop his head and he was wearing feminine clothing.

Kay fumbled in her purse and gave him an unopened pack of cigarettes.

Dane was troubled, "I wish you wouldn't do that. He scares the hell out of me."

"I really feel that he would never harm me. His only history of violence was to himself. He's tried to commit suicide four times."

"Why in the world do you know so much about him?"

Kay stopped and looked back at Minney, "I was only here a few days when he was transferred from Elmira Psychiatric. He was hearing voice commanding him to kill himself. Despite his size, he looked so gentle when I did his admission papers that I never forgot him. I just know he wouldn't hurt me."

Dane looked back at the man. He was standing motionless, broom resting on the ground, staring after them.

The Old Pier was awash with employees from the hospital as Kay and Dane entered. There was a short wait for tables so when they spied Donna and Nugent at the bar, they joined them.

The sergeant was in civilian clothes. His face was beet red, apparently he had been at the bar for some time. Donna and he were sipping martinis and offered Kay and Dane the same. The restaurant was noisy with the hospital employees who were celebrating the ending of the murder investigation.

Dane hesitated, "God, I'd love one but I can't handle them any more. I'll have a light beer."

Kay nodded, "Me too. I'm going to the funeral in the morning for the Caples girl and there is a team treatment meeting right after."

A table became vacant and their names were called. They carried their drinks to the table and as they sat down, Kay looked back at the bar, "I wish Donna would slow down her romance with Nugent. He's a heavy drinker and she seems to be trying to keep up with him."

Dane remembered his younger days when drinking and violence seemed to go with the blue uniform and didn't answer.

After dinner, as they walked to their cars, the heavy screen mesh obscured the figure in white gazing down on them with burning eyes from the window of the Citadel.

⇒ Chapter 22

Drack was on the Caples Girl's treatment team and had been treating her for years. When the mobile Crisis team brought her to the hospital this last time, he was reassigned to her case. He forced himself to attend the Caples girl's burial he knew it would have looked odd if he didn't.

Belial and Lew were with him at the ceremonies murmuring incoherently and occasionally breaking into laughter. They became raucous when the clergyman was finishing the death prayers, mocking his gestures and incantations. The Reverend John Graham, his round face solemn, began his prayer for the dead. He started with the usual address to the family, then realized there was none. He then commented on the brutal way the Caples girl died. The crowd around the grave site was stunned when the Reverend reminded them that the old testament bible taught them that redemption was only possible through the shedding of blood. Belial broke into raucous laughter, jeering the man and promising more redemption for the hospital community. Lew was recklessly urging Drack to follow the preacher and give him the redemption he seemed to relish.

When the services were ended, Drack left the cemetery as swiftly as he could. He made his rounds at the hospital and finished on the eighth floor. As he was taking the elevator down, it stopped at

146

the third floor and a slim young patient got on. She smiled and recognizing him, said hello and pushed a button for the first floor. The elevator was one of the few in the hospital that went all the way down to the tunnels. The door opened at the first floor and the girl stepped out and turned to say something to Drack. Belial roared to take her. Drack quickly looked out to an empty lobby and grabbed the startled girl and dragged her back into the elevator.

When she started to scream, he put his hand over her mouth, and pushed the down button. He strangled her with his other hand until she was unconscious. When the elevator stopped at the basement, he picked her up and carried her through the catacombs to his home. Laying her on his operating table, he gazed down at her black hair tumbling around her face. It was his first victim that didn't have blonde hair. As she stirred, he felt the heat rising in his groin. He stripped off his clothes and picked one of the surgical knives from a rack on the wall and slit her dress, bra and panties down the middle. As he was leaning over her, she awoke and began screaming.

Kay and Dane were the center of a group that walked briskly from the grave. The cold November wind freshened by dampness from the Sound had everyone shivering.

Dane broke the silence, "The Reverend sure didn't do his homework. He should have known that the poor kid didn't have any family."

Donna agreed, "He's an idiot. I know he was referring to Christ dying on a cross but he should have been aware what we've been going through at the hospital."

They walked in silence until they left the cemetery. Dane looked back at all the tiny markers, "There's hundreds of graves in there, most of them with no birth date, just a name and the day they died. It's pretty depressing."

Donna said, "If you want to see something sad go up behind that stretch of woods. There's a mass grave there that contains the remains of over three hundred people that were dug up when they started to build the high school in the forties. They were in unidentified graves and the only marker is that big cross that was put up by the local churches."

Dane was incredulous, "Nobody claimed their bodies?"

Donna shook her head, "Some of the patients were sent out here from the city. For the most part, they were immigrants who spoke little English. At that time, the hospital was staffed almost entirely by Irish immigrants who put down the names they thought the patients told them. The names were often misspelled. Anyone trying to locate them would have a difficult problem."

"My God! That is sad."

_____

The treatment meeting started right after the funeral of the Caples girl. Dr. Liebman was in Albany on one of his political visits and Dr. Abbott was chairing the meeting. He cleared his throat and began, "Dr. Liebman wants us to cover these five cases today and due to the funeral, we are short of time so will have to hurry along. The first case is that of Thomas Loretto, a single white male of Italian extraction. He has a long history of substance abuse, although he continually denies any addiction to alcohol or drugs. His risk factors are two suicide attempts while a patient at the Northport VA facility." Dr. Abbott looked up from the transcript and commented, "Unfortunately, these attempts have not been documented by the VA. He was released from that facility after their special release team felt that he was no longer suicidal and his volatile behavior were no longer present. The client reported compliance with outpatient medication but this was doubtful since he never seemed to run out of medication. He expressed his intention to finish college and to become a substance abuse counselor."

Dr. Abbot looked up impatiently as several of the group snickered. One of them said in sotto voice, "I remember him. He's one of those professional veterans."

Dr. Abbott said, "Please! The client felt strongly that being that the Government, due to the aggressive military training he received, owed him full disability benefits. Mr. Loretto became frustrated when he discovered he was not evaluated as fully disabled. He lives with his girlfriend and her two young sons. He reported himself to be very active in Veteran Support Groups. His recent admission was caused by him threatening to shoot a former employer. The employer called the Suffolk County Police and then Mr. Loretto also threatened the police in front of witnesses. The patient fled but was picked up while attempting to enter one of the adult homes where he occasionally lived."

Dr. Abbott threw the transcript angrily down on the lectern, "What the hell was this guy ever doing at an adult home? What bothers me is that the treatment team has put under Discharge Planning that he is to be put into a community based residence when stable. Then he is to be followed up at a mental health clinic for medication and supportive counseling."

One of the medical doctors stood up, "Hold on Jim. I signed that transcript. What the hell can we do with him. We're closing wards and simply don't have the room or resources to keep him here."

"Dr. Kenny, I know it's not your fault or anyone else on the team. The sad part is that there is no place to keep him and I'm sure he's going to kill someone some day."

Kay thought as she scribbled her notes, no wonder we have so many serial killers in this country.

Abbott continued, "Now we have the President's plan to end homelessness. You all know about the idiot son of the former governor who landed a patronage job with HUD. This genius has written a report requesting that the government throw billions of dollars into the government's assistance budget. The plan focuses mainly on federally sponsored homes for the homeless. This cretin feels that most of our homeless are living on the street because of poverty and then drift into drugs and alcohol. Everyone in our profession knows that it is the other way around. I recently attended a conference in Atlanta and everyone in attendance ripped this report."

One of the psychiatrists stood up, "Wasn't there a paper on the Portland experiment discussed there as well?"

Abbott nodded, "A member of the delegation from Portland, Oregon gave a report on what they are doing to attack their homeless problems. It's a concerted effort by social workers who are deputized by the police department to take druggies and drunks against their will, to sobering up stations. They are held there until sober. When that occurs, specially trained social workers, like our people here, try to convince them to go into rehab programs. Then, they take their patients thorough detox, residential treatment centers at their mental hospitals and then into alcohol and drug free housing. The final step is to put them into permanent housing, get them jobs and back into society. Guess what? It's still working. The homeless have virtually disappeared from the streets of Portland."

One of the audience asked, "What are they doing about the patients who are released into society and needs further medication as an outpatient? That is the biggest hole in all these programs. Once they are free and feel well enough to stop taking their medication, they often will slip back into their illness."

"Portland has a second step in the program, particularly for the violent prone, that if they stop taking their medication, they face being readmitted to a psychiatric hospital. It's the law and it's enforced."

Dr. Abbott said, "We're wasting our time discussing this. It's a great program but we will never get it in place in this state."

The group hurriedly discussed the rest of the cases and finished up just in time to close their offices. As they left the premises, the overcast sky started to let drops of snow skate lazily down over the Island.

➣ Chapter 23

The weeks passed quietly after the death of Olsen and Drack was careful to keep himself under heavy doses of Kloningin. He also started on smaller doses of Prozac and cut down on the cocaine, using it only when the need became intense.

He began to lay his plans to leave the hospital and find a new life. He would change his appearance and get a new identity. There was enough files on deceased patients that would contain birth records, social security numbers and other vital information that would enable him to slip into another identity. His inheritance and the plan gave him a sense of security and an exuberance that puzzled his co-workers.

He placed his name with several national real estate agencies and carefully perused the literature he received from them. Among the many booklets he received was a portrait of a small hospital in the country, between Marlboro and Boston.

Drack was intrigued with the idea of setting up a private mental hospital where he could continue his collections without fear of discovery. Of course, he would take his current collections with him. However, before he could leave he had to erase some of the witnesses to his past. The professor had to be the first to go. Lately the man began to respond to treatment and having lucid *moments to the extent that he was answering some questions in full sentences.*

Recently, a decision was reached to move him to one of the halfway houses on the grounds. Drack was fearful that the professor, while in one of his therapy sessions would blurt out his remembering the sight of the killing of the Wainwright girl.

Drack couldn't get near the man. When they were in the same room, the professor would become agitated and immediately leave. Thus far, the staff was puzzled by his behavior and hadn't connected Drack with the incidents.

The early winter storm laid a blanket of snow on the grounds and made pedestrian traffic difficult except on the shoveled paths and roads.

The professor had been in Options house for a week and was rapidly coming out of his shell. Bits and pieces of the debris of the fallen walls of his mind began to disappear. Memories of his childhood outside Philadelphia were the first to return. Pictures of his parents and brothers and sisters came back into focus, although their names escaped him at times. It was considered a good omen that his long range memory was returning and that he was able to vocalize his remembrances.

He sat in the morning therapy session at option house with the other patients and attempted to focus his attention on the conversation flowing between patients and the therapy aide. It was as though he was at the end of a tunnel, where he could see and hear the other patients but he was too far away to touch them. His gaze wandered across the room stopping at the big picture window that looked out on the grounds. The latest snowfall left a clean sheet of white over the trees and ground. The tunnel closed and he was back in the slum neighborhood of North 10th Street in Philadelphia.

The dark faces of his brothers and sisters were vague and he couldn't connect names with them, but his father and mother swam into focus, his father's figure was blurred and indistinct but his mother was sharp and strong, her round tired face always a comfort in his struggle to achieve. She was the one who went into the abandoned row houses and cut out the sections of linoleum to line their shoes when there wasn't enough money to have them repaired.

She was the accountant that took the father's small paycheck as a street car conductor in North Philadelphia and paid the bills. The wages she earned on her knees at night, cleaning the floors of the office buildings in Downtown Philadelphia was put in the bank as a college fund for the children.

It didn't matter how tired as she was, she would take him to the Quaker free library on a Saturday morning to fuel his insatiable reading habit. He quickly fell in love with the masters of literature, particularly those of the Romantic Period. His hero was Byron, that tortured soul whose lifestyle matched the Professor's inner conflict.

His passion for poetry led him to the sonnets of Shakespeare and from there to the great writer's plays. His favorite was Richard the Third, although he disagreed with Shakespeare's depiction of the king as a villain.

His mother's pride in his consistently high grades in high school was equaled by his amazing skill at basketball. He received an avalanche of scholarships from colleges all over the country. His mother was indignant that the offers were all for his ability as a basketball player and not for his grades.

His love of reading led him to make the choice of English as his master. He chose an offer of an athletic scholarship from Temple University so as to be near his mother. As he progressed through Temple, he became further distanced from his brothers and sisters who took to crime in the streets of Philadelphia. His only link to the family was his mother and he couldn't tell even her of his growing problem.

It started in his first basketball practice in the college gym. It was the first time he was in a communal shower since high school and found himself aroused by the naked bodies of his teammates. He was embarrassed at his sudden erection and hastily hid it with a towel. Thereafter he made it a point to be the last one in the shower. When it happened in high school, he never used the shower, choosing instead to change into his street clothes and go home while his teammates were showering.

After graduation he fled Philadelphia and after receiving his masters degree, taught in a high school in the New York inner city educational system. His devotion to teaching and his athletic record at Temple, aided him in reaching the youth of the city.

Soon his success brought him to Hofstra and the happiest times of his life. He was a popular teacher with the students and well thought of by the faculty. The suburban campus was heaven to him after the years in a metropolitan area. The theaters on campus fed his intellectual hunger and it was at one of the musicals that he met Michael. The boy was a dancer in the play, South Pacific, and they met and fell in love at a cast party after the last performance.

His world was shattered when they were involved in a nasty scandal when their affair was discovered. The media publicity and his discharge from the college and subsequent suicide by the boy broke him. He spiraled down into a well of despondency and felt his mind slowly collapsing in on itself, each crash shutting off the outside world.

He started as he heard his name being called, "Professor, we all benefit only when the group as a whole participates. How do you feel about Karen's problem?"

The professor looked at the group, each in turn slowly from one person to another, ignoring the snickers of his neighbors. He dumbly shook his head at the aide.

The aide marked something in her notepad , "Alright, we'll go on to the next question. Does anyone have an event they have recently experienced?"

The professor was relieved when several hands shot up and attention was diverted from him.

The sudden noise of a snowplow passing the window on the road outside Options house brought his attention to the outside again. He stiffened at first as an indistinct figure seemed to rise out of the sheets of falling snow. It was the evil one. The scene of him kneeling over the half naked girl and strangling her flashed to the forefront of his mind, he leaped to his feet, knocking over his chair and began to peal scream after scream.

→ Chapter 24

A frightened Drack hurried back to the safety of his home. The sudden reaction of the Professor when he spied him through the window settled any questions as to when the professor must die. It had to be soon and done in a fashion to keep suspicion away from him or to even look like a murder. He reached the sanctuary of his home and hurried to his collection room and sat in the chair and closed his eyes and let Belial come to him.

"You'll have to wait until he's placed back in one of the wards where we can dispose of him."

Drack nodded, "But how? Even if they return him to one of the wards, he's not one of my patients. It would look suspicious if I were to go into a ward after him. I have no reason to be even near the man. Besides, I can't get close to him. As soon as he sees me he either runs away or makes a commotion. Sooner or later someone will get the connection."

"Have no fear. This latest outburst will put him back in the wards soon where we can get to him. Remember Mr. Cofeld?"

Cofeld was a patient of Drack's who urinated in his bed and on any furniture near him. He had a constant erection and would couple with willing female patients in hallways, wards or any place available.

Once when Drack's attention was diverted, Cofeld urinated on his legs much to the amusement of the other patients. That night Drack substituted a strong stimulus for the man's medicine. Cofeld died of a massive heart attack during the night.

Kay hurried down the hall and entered her office to find a smiling Donna waiting for her with a container of coffee. She asked Donna, "Has anybody heard from the Kiernan girl?"

"No. My sergeant says that her parents are worried that she's taken off again. Apparently, she's done this in the past. She has an alcohol problem that nobody caught when she was hired here."

"It is a little scary, considering what's been going on here recently."

Donna shrugged, "I haven't seen much of you since you started romancing Dane." She looked shrewdly at Kay, "You look like you've dropped a few pounds and your color is the best it's been since you started working here. I'd say you finally started having a healthy sex life."

Kay felt her face redden, "I'm really happy, Donna. For the first time I feel that I have a future again. I have someone who really cares what I do and think."

"It might help your mental attitude if you can keep losing weight. I jog on the boardwalk in the state park after work. Why don't you run with me?"

Kay hesitated, "I never was into the physical thing. The only exercise I liked was swimming as a young girl. Besides, when Don left, I took up smoking again. I'd probable collapse after ten feet."

Donna kept cajoling Kay until she finally agreed to bring in a jogging suit and running shoes the next day.

The next night after work, Kay joined Donna on the boardwalk and was surprised at the number of people, old and young, jogging or walking. Fortunately, a week of warm weather evaporated most of the snow from the boardwalk and it was clear and dry. They were able to extend their running well into November.

The first night of running was particularly painful. She quickly became breathless and experienced severe pains in her chest. Donna advised her to walk and then jog a few feet, stopping as soon as her breathing became laborious. It helped and she was able to complete a half mile the first night. The running became gradually easier and when she stopped smoking, was able to increase the distances and keep up with Donna.

They were a picture on the boardwalk, blonde ponytails bobbing from side to side above their jogging suits. Kay was thrilled when the day came when she could fit into the same size dress as Donna and also began wearing a nurse's white dress to work. Co-workers soon began calling them the Gold Dust twins.

Dane complained ruefully that Kay was spending more time with Donna than with him but smilingly endorsed the activity because of the improvement in Kay, mentally and physically. When she invited him to join them in their runs, he quickly accepted although the pounding on his knee left him in pain after every run. For the first time since Anna's death he was able to sleep through the night.

It was after one such run and the three were walking back to their cars when Dane asked Kay, "Have you found anyone who knows anything about the name of Belial?"

Kay shook her head, "No. My friend in Personnel said no one by that name ever worked here."

Donna broke in, "Who's Belial?"

Kay answered, "Jim and one of the aides heard Olsen repeating the name the day he was shot. I checked all my listings and we don't have a patient by that name."

Donna said, "Why don't you go to the hospital archive library and check their old lists. They have files on all the patients records in their computer that have ever been here since they opened the place."

Dane and Kay followed Donna's car out of the parking lot of the park and went back onto the hospital grounds so that Dane could pick up his car. As they were passing the hospital library, Dane impulsively swung into the parking lot.

He looked quizzically at Kay, "Lets go in and see if we can find anything on Belial."

"I don't think that anyone is there at this time. It usually closes at four thirty right on the button."

As they were getting out of their car, a woman came out of the building and was preparing to lock the door. Dane called out to her to wait. The woman turned around with a surprised look, but waited until they got to the door.

"Hi Kay. Hello Mr. Dane. What are you two doing here so late? I thought I was the only one working overtime."

"We just wanted to look up one of our past patients in the computer. Could you wait a few minutes"

The woman shook her head, "No. But I can lock you in and you can exit through the side door. It has a crash bar that will lock the door behind you."

They entered the computer room and Kay quickly accessed the patient list. The program listed the patients by the years and in order to find a name, the program called for the operator to enter a name when the prompt," SEARCH" came on the screen. Kay entered the name Belial and waited while the old computer scanned its memory.

The screen read, "Belial. Access Lew Thomas"

➤ Chapter 25

Drack sat in his car staring in astonishment at Kay's car sitting in the parking lot of the library. She was always so punctual as were all the employees at leaving the grounds when their shift was up. He heard Belial softly urging him to investigate. "This is our chance to get the bitch alone. Hurry!"

He got out of the car as the first flakes of snow fell heralding the arrival of the blizzard that the media had been warning Long Island about for days.

He went to the front door of the building and gently tried the knob and found it locked. The roaring in his head became louder and he responded by furiously shaking the handle of the door. Desperately he looked about to find something to pry the door open with and spied the outline of an old abandoned building through the snow. With the voices of Belial and Lew screaming in his head, Drack bolted for his car and drove to the old building.

Taking a flashlight from his glove compartment, he ran into the lobby and down to the basement. He was able to tug open the door to the catacombs and wended his way to the basement of the library and went up to the first floor and cautiously peered down the deserted corridor. The light in the computer room drew his attention and he soundlessly made his way to the door. He looked in and saw Kay with her back to him, accessing the computer and froze. She was peering intently at the screen. The heading on the green CRT said in large capital letters that the file belonged to Lew Thomas.

The voices of Belial and Thomas were hysterical and never louder. "Kill the bitch. No. Bring her to the collection room, we'll do her there. Slowly."

Kay and Dane heard the rattling of the front door and he patted Kay, "Keep searching while I go see who's at the door. On my way back, I'll use the john. That is, if I can find it in the dark."

Kay nodded and had the computer change menus and accessed the file on Lew Thomas.

QUEENS PARK PSYCHIATRIC CENTER
PATIENT CARE ASSESSMENT - PART 1

PATIENT NAME; THOMAS, LEW   APRIL 10, 1928

BLDGING. /WARD # 22/217

ADMISSION DATA

This is a 31 year old single white male admitted on violent status when he was referred by Judge John G. Clary of the Suffolk county criminal court because of criminal assault, agitation, and violent behavior at his trial. Patient has been complaining of hearing command voices ordering him to hurt himself and also an employer who refused to give him a job.

Arrested by Suffolk County police after attempting to kill a passerby whom he said had been following him with intent to harm.

CULTURAL/ETHNIC STATUS;

Patient is of Anglo/American Descent.

PERSONAL/SOCIAL HISTORY;

Patient is single with his parents (biological) both having a history of mental illness. Patient has a history of drug and alcohol abuse.

PRESENT MEDICAL HISTORY; None available at this time.

Kay was about to flip the screen to the next page when a gasp caused her to turn around. A shadowy figure in a long white hospital gown was standing in the doorway. Kay screamed and the figure fled as the sound of pounding feet could be heard in the hallway and Dane shouting her name.

Dane rushed into the room and comforted a shaken Kay, "Who or what in hell was that?"

"I don't know. His face was in the dark and I couldn't see him."

A door slammed at the end of the hall. Dane and Kay went down the hall, cautiously testing office doors as they went. They were all locked as were all doors throughout the hospital. They came to the big metal door which led to the staircase leading to other floors.

Dane produced his master key and tried the door. He pushed it open and let it slam shut behind them. The noise seemed to be loud enough to be heard throughout the hospital. He nodded, "This is the one we heard. I'm going down to see what I can find. Do you want to wait here?"

Kay shook her head vigorously, "I want to get out of here, but if you're going down there, I'm going with you."

They found the light switch and flicked it to the on position. The heavy layer of dust made it obvious that the stairs were never used. There was a clear set of footprints going up and down the stairs leading to the basement.

As they slowly descended, Dane muttered, "I wish to hell I had my gun."

They reached the basement, passing row upon row of boxes of files. There was a set of footprints leading to another door and Dane cautiously forced it open. The light from the stairwell shed some light into the tunnel, but only for a few feet.

Dane closed the door saying, "I'm not going in there with you and without a flashlight. I'll come back tomorrow with a couple of my men and see where those footprints go."

"Thank God! Let's get out of here."

"Do you mind if we stop at the computer and print up that info on Thomas that you were looking at?"

Kay was miserable and frightened, but nodded.

She scrolled the computer down to the last page of the file on Thomas and prepared to print out the report. The page was a discharge form. Dane grabbed Kay by the arm as she was preparing to hit the print control.

"Jesus, look at that."

Kay read the page aloud.

RELEASE/TERMINATION SUMMARY   THOMAS, LOUIS

PATIENT NUMBER; 72122   WARD/UNIT 17/21

FACILITY QUEENS PARK PSYCHIATRIC CENTER

EVENT; DISCHARGE   REASON; DEATH

DISCHARGE DATA:

This was a 31 year old white, single male that was discharged due to death by suicide after murdering three young nurses. Against all warnings Thomas was permitted a treatment pass to attend a workshop. This, despite his violent behavior and uncooperative attitude while at the hospital. Dr. Gutterman reported incidents of screaming, yelling, banging feet and with assaultive tendencies towards the female patients of the facility. He made many references to hearing voices telling him to kill. His latest sessions made reference many times to his master, "Belial" ordering sacrifices to be made in his name. Thomas consistently refused to identify Belial but Dr. Gutterman researched the name and found that it is a word that occurs a few times in the Hebrew Bible and other Jewish literature of the Greco-Roman period. In later literature it is referred to as one of Satan's titles. When Dr. Gutterman brought this information up in a session with Thomas, the patient attacked Dr. Gutterman and almost killed him if it hadn't been for the intercession of the aides.

DISCHARGE DATE: 4/23/31

Kay printed the file as Dane thought aloud, "What the hell does the killing of three nurses and the suicide of a patient have to do with Olsen and murders committed almost seventy years later?"

⇛ Chapter 26

A shaken Drack crouched in the darkness and watched Dane and the bitch as they stood in the arc of light and shivered as he heard the man say he was coming back the next day to search. After they closed the door and he heard the receding footsteps ascending the stairs, he turned the flashlight on and removed his hospital gown. He quickly retraced his steps and using the gown as a mop carefully erased the footprints and backed all the way to the abandoned building eliminating his traces. All the while, Belial and Lew screaming that he had to disappear from the hospital. But first he had to kill the professor and then make the bitch disappear.

The blizzard hit Long Island with screaming winds ranging from sixty to seventy miles an hour. It was a slow moving storm that settled over the Island for days. Power was knocked out in hundreds of thousands of homes and people were forced to evacuate their houses and seek shelter in emergency centers.

The hospital was fortunate in that it had it's own power plant for heat and light. The biggest problem was shortage of personnel. People who lived off the grounds were unable to get to work the next day. Most were unable to reach their departments by phone. There was only one switchboard operator who was hapless enough to have come out of her office when the storm began to find one of her tires was flat.

She, like some of the nurses and doctors on the night shift were doing yeoman service keeping the hospital going. Some of the people who lived on the grounds in Doctors Row were unable or unwilling to make it to their wards.

It was a dangerous situation for those who were working in the hospital, since the rule of thumb was that when the wards were open there had to be a one on one ratio to personnel/patients. Medical care and most psychiatric treatment were suspended.

The hospital had an ample supply of food in its storage lockers and cafeteria to feed everyone. The problem was to feed the wards without someone getting killed. All available personnel were used to herd the patients in shifts to the cafeteria to feed them.

The violent wards containing the multiple killers were fed by carts and trays of food, person by person. People unaccustomed to being in close contact with these cases broke and ran when the howling and threats erupted.

Only the strongest and most experienced were allowed to enter these wards at night to give the patients their medication. These exhausted aides, doctors and nurses had to go from ward to ward to feed and medicate the patients until two in the morning.

Cots were put up in the cafeteria and people fell into their bunks at night fully dressed, to arise three of four hours later in order to start the process all over again.

The storm hovered over Long Island for four days and dropped over fifty inches of snow on the hapless Island.

The hospital, staff and patients was as isolated as though the buildings were dropped onto a deserted island.

Chapter 27

Drack worked tirelessly in the wards assisting in feeding and medicating the patients. He was leading a group of patients down to the cafeteria and as he led his group into the room he met the Professor being led out after finishing his dinner.

The Professor screamed, broke and ran. Two of the tired aides gave chase as he raced up the stairs to his ward, swearing and promising that when they caught him that he was going on sheet restraint and a heavy dose of Prozac.

Drack smiled and heard Belial chuckling at the plan. The tired aides of Drack's group never noticed that he had left. Actually, few caretakers in each group knew one another since they came from diverse professions and being exhausted, cared less.

Drack went to the catacombs and took the tunnel to the door leading to the basement of his home. He lay down and set his alarm for two o'clock.

He was awake before the alarm went off and dressing, he went back down into the tunnel and arrived back at Building 22 before three o'clock.

There wasn't a soul moving about and he easily accessed the medicine closet and quickly found what he was searching for. It was Marcane, a powerful stimulant that was given sparingly to assist weak hearts. Taking a bottle and a dosage dispenser with him, he mounted the stairs to the professor's ward. There were no aides on duty and he used his master key to enter the ward. There wasn't a sound in the unit except for the noises emanating from the heavily sedated patients as he moved silently down to the professor's bed.

Pouring the Marcane into the dispenser, he gently lifted the professor's head up and began pouring the liquid into his mouth. The professor, being accustomed to taking medication at all hours never opened his eyes as he obediently drank the dose.

The powerful drug took only a few seconds to attack his heart. The professor awoke as convulsions wracked his body and he screamed for help just before the first blow to his chest left him breathless. His stomach was on fire as though heavy with indigestion. The other patients although heavily sedated, heard his cries for help and made unintelligible noise in response to his cries for aid. They surrounded his bed, some laughing but making no effort to remove the sheet restraints. Drack moved to the far end of the ward closest to the door, wanting to be sure none of the patients were inclined to seek help.

None of the patients moved as he turned to leave, giggling with Belial and Lew joining him in his merriment. As he opened the door, a rustle of sheets from a cot drew his attention. It was Popeye, glaring at him with eyes filled with hate and fear.

The professor didn't die at once, but had multiple heart attacks during the night destroying the lower part of the heart and then eventually its walls. Finally, near dawn, his heart virtually exploded and when the aides came to feed the patients in the ward in the morning, he was dead.

The storm lessened enough on the fifth day so that road crews were able to clear some lanes on most of the major arteries on the Island.

Side roads were impassable with drifts up to thirty feet and stalled, abandoned cars littering the streets. The public was asked to stay at home unless they had an emergency. The snow kept falling.

Dane awoke the fifth morning of the storm to the view of Dolan sitting on his chest. They stared eyeball to eyeball until Dane gave up and groaning, threw the covers aside. He was bundled up in a sweat suit over thermal underwear and padded to the kitchen, his feet feeling the cold through two pairs of heavy socks. The rumbling noise of a snowplow outside the house drew him to the front picture window and he peered out.

The snow had let up a bit and visibility improved to where he could barely see the front of his lawn. He cursed as he watched the plow throw snow on top of the huge drift in front of his driveway. It was going to be weeks after the storm was over before he would be able to get his car out of the garage.

Shivering, he lit the kerosene heater and grimacing at the pungent odor of the fumes, put a pot of water on top of the heater. Opening the sliding door to the patio he brought in the pail hanging on the wall. It contained the last of his milk and cold cuts.

He made a sandwich out of the cold cuts and when the water came to a slow boil made a cup of instant coffee. He poured some of the milk into his coffee and poured the rest into a saucer for Dolan. Staring at the cat, he remembered his girls asking him why the name Dolan. They had laughed when he said that it was after a friend of his from his neighborhood in Brooklyn who had been the first of his crowd to go to college. The man was an intelligent, affable friend when sober but when intoxicated became pugnacious and challenged anyone, friend or stranger to a fight.

A poor fighter when sober, he was helpless when drunk. Normally, those who knew him would simply push him away but when a fight was impossible to avoid, one punch would decide the issue.

As soon as Dane had brought the cat home, it developed a feisty nature and when let outside attacked every cat in sight and would come home with pieces of his ear missing and his nose tracked with scratches. He never won a fight. The girls laughed with delight when he told the story and loved the animal all the more.

When the girls died, he considered getting rid of the cat but changed his mind, remembering that it was a link to his loved ones. When Kay and her children made one of their rare visits to his house, they fell in love with the cat and the story.

Dane went to the phone and listened for a dial tone. The phones were still dead. The batteries on his portable radio had gone dead the day before. He had no idea as to what was going on in the world. As he hung up the phone, he glanced out the window and saw a heavily bundled figure trudging along the top of the snow embankment, sinking into the top where the surface had softened.

It started Dane thinking of bundling up and walking over to Kay's house. He quickly rejected the idea. She lived two miles past the hospital. Instead, he decided on going to the hospital first and warming himself there. He knew they had their own power plant and would have warm food and heat.

And people.

Dane packed extra clothes, and put all the cat food that was in the house into a large bowl for Dolan and stepped out into the storm. A gust of wind struck him and took his breath away. He had a difficult time just making it to the end of his driveway and faced the huge snow bank that blocked him in.

A stand of trees separated his property from his neighbors and the branches provided a ladder he could climb that would put him on top of the snow bank. Climbing the tree with difficulty, he reached a branch that allowed him to peer over the bank and tentatively put one foot out testing the firmness of the snow. He immediately sank up to his thigh. He would have to jump and slide down the other side of the snow bank. He hesitated, thinking, that once he was out in the street, he wouldn't be able to get back in to the house.

Taking a deep breath he leaped out as far as he could. The snow on the reverse side of the bank was firm from the freezing wind and he skidded and slid his way into the street.

The route from his home to the hospital was on fairly level ground all the way to the road where the hospital was located. There was little to break the force of the fierce gusts that threw particles of stinging snow into his exposed face. He passed blocked side streets, some with abandoned cars blocking the crosswalks and followed his street onto the main highway.

A caravan of snowplows passed him with a State Trooper's car bringing up the rear, it's dome light flashing. It stopped and the driver rolled down his window. "Where the hell do you think you're going?"

"I'm the security officer at the hospital and I'm trying to make my way in."

"Get in. We're going to be crossing Williams Street as we plow. You'll only have a short walk to the hospital."

As they followed the snowplows, the trooper told Dane that another storm was right behind the current one. Each town on the Island was basically on its own. Communications, power and light were down from Queens to Montauk Point. People were abandoning their homes all over the Island and seeking shelter at predetermined safe emergency areas.

Exhausted linemen had temporarily given up repairing fallen lines. As fast as they put them up, tree branches, heavily laden with snow, blown onto the lines would bring them down again. The trooper said they were finding people frozen to death in houses and cars all over the Island.

"You're lucky I came along. Once you get there, you better figure that you're there for at least the next ten days. Until it stops snowing, that hospital might as well be on an island in the middle of the ocean."

When they reached Williams street, Dane got out and floundered down the street through knee deep snow onto the grounds of the hospital.

There were people from the hospital clearing a path from the Admission building to the parking lot and Dane made the final two hundred feet a little easier.

Dane thankfully entered the main doors of Admissions and stood for a moment savoring the warmth.

He was surprised to learn that he was not the first of the hospital employees to make it to work. Dedicated employees who lived in the vicinity walked in. Some from as far as a mile away.

An enterprising old timer produced a map of the old tunnels that connected the buildings to one another. Doors that were locked and forgotten were opened to the tunnels so that the staff could get from building to building. Copies of the map were made and passed out to key personnel. Powerful flashlights were given out with the maps and teams appointed to examine the tunnels and markers put up identifying each building and its doors. Battery driven flood lamps were placed at the foot of the stairs leading to the tunnels with instructions that they were to be left on until the party using the tunnel returned. Old oil fired hurricane lamps were discovered in one of the supply rooms and placed in strategic areas throughout the catacombs.

Dane personally led several of the groups through the tunnels and began to feel as though they were getting a handle on organizing the staff.

Telephone service was re-established on the grounds and a command post set up in Admissions. A strike force comprised of a medical doctor, a psych and two burly aides had been set up to travel to hot spots throughout the grounds.

Dr. Abbott was leading one such group to building 22 and took a wrong turn, "What the hell is that odor?"

The aide next to him shrugged, "Probably an animal that came down out of the storm and died. I'm more concerned as to where the hell we are."

While the aide was reading the map, Abbott ventured a few feet on up the tunnel and rounded a curve. He recoiled in horror at the three butchered bodies that were strewn on the ground. "Jesus Christ!"

The rest of the group who came up behind him in answer to his cry stopped, transfixed at the sight. Abbott herded them away from the scene, "Lets get to a phone and have Admissions call the police."

Dane carrying a container of coffee had just walked into the command post in Admissions when the strike force telephoned of the discovery of the bodies.

Dane telephoned Detective Dicks at Yaphank and was surprised to find him in his office. "Hello Jim. This is Dane over at the hospital."

"Hi. What are you doing there? I'd have thought you'd be home watching old movies."

"On what? I woke up this morning with a hell of a case of cabin fever and decided to walk here. I just got in and one of the doctors called and told me they found three more bodies in one of the tunnels under the hospital. I'm getting ready to go down there now."

Dicks was silent for a moment, "There isn't a damn thing I can do except file a report when you call me back. There isn't anything moving on the highways except snowplows and emergency equipment." He laughed dryly, "I know we can't move but the bad guys can't either."

Dane laughed and hung up, promising to call him back when he had more information.

Dane and an MD were led to the three bodies in the tunnel. The Doctor rose after examining the corpses and said, "They've been dead at least three months. That's only a rough guess because animals have been at them. Rats, I guess. It will take a forensic expert to give you a better time. I can tell you that they were slashed or stabbed to death."

Dane said, "This must be more of Olsen's work." He had one of the aides call Admissions and to have a party come back with body bags to bring the corpses to the temporary mortuary.

He examined the wallets that were found on the bodies and not recognizing the names, put them in his pocket.

He had just arrived back at Admissions when Kay and Donna walked in, laughing and covered with snow.

⇒ Chapter 28

Drack went into a cyclonic fury, fueled by fear when he saw the activity in his tunnels. He carefully bolted the door from his collection room to the catacombs and did what he could to hide the evidence of the entrance to his house from the tunnels. At first, he curtailed his movements in the tunnels until he realized that there was so much traffic during the day, he could move as freely as before. His only problem was the curious looks he received when he was seen traveling alone at night. The evenings were still his because once the patients were settled in for the night, traffic dwindled to a few teams hurrying back to their base.

When he learned that the bodies of the three men were discovered he felt the walls of his mind closing in. He was certain that there had been no danger of their being found until he left the hospital.

None of the drugs were able to completely keep Belial or Lew under control. Drack was able to go about his duties with a calm detachment but he was now a puppet under the strings of Belial, Lew was rarely heard from. That night, they happened on a young therapy worker going alone, very late to her sleeping quarters. It meant no more to him than taking a breath when they brought her through the tunnels to their collection room. It was a good night. Her screams of pain harmonized to the thundering music of Wagner.

Dane stared at Kay in amazement, "What are you two doing here?"

Kay replied, "If I hadn't gotten out of that house, I would have shot my kids sooner or later. When Donna called and told me she was going to walk in, I took the kids over to my sister's house and came in with Donna. I'm surprised to see you. You live a lot further away than I do."

Kay watched Donna walk away, "Eddie was driving me crazy. My ex called to see how we were doing during the storm and had a long talk with Eddie. He wants him to come out and visit him in California."

"Let him visit his father. It might take some of the heat from us."

She gave him a troubled look and went to join Donna.

Dane watched the two women go off to report in to Admissions and felt a sense of uneasiness. As he hefted the wallets of the dead men he wished that Kay had stayed home.

Dane dialed Dicks' direct line and he answered immediately. The man sounded tired, "Hi Dane. Anything on the three bodies?"

"Yeah. I've got their wallets. Their all locals."

Dane gave him their names and addresses and asked him to call him back if he had anything on them.

One of the young therapy aides came in with a troubled look on her face, "Mr. Dane, my roommate, Pat Kiernan, didn't sleep in her bed last night. Her cot is next to mine in the upstairs rec room."

"She must be in the hospital somewhere. There's over five feet of snow outside. I'll have them check the other buildings and have her get back to you."

The girl left and Dane went over to the command post and asked the operator to have all the buildings ask the Kiernan girl to contact Admissions.

He was still in the command post when Dicks called back. "We have dossiers on all three of those birds. They all have records dating back to juvenile court. They apparently have recently entered the drug business. One of the cops in your precinct feels sure that they are pushing. It's possible that this is a drug deal gone wrong or they could have run into our boy Olsen when they shouldn't have."

Dane agreed, "I think they belong to Olsen. Most dealers use guns. These guys were all butchered the same way those girls were. It just seems odd that he changed his pattern and killed the three men."

Dicks sighed. "At this point in time it doesn't make a damn bit of difference. I can't get out of here until the storm stops and they clear away some of the snow. Just put them on ice until we can get there."

Dane was about to end the conversation when Dicks spoke again, "I just had a thought. Why don't you call that big sergeant from the county cops? What's his name? Nugent? He's from Queens Park and I can have him assigned to the hospital until the storm breaks."

"OK, thanks I can use the help." Dane hesitated, "One of the young therapy aids is missing and I've got people looking for her."

Dicks groaned, "She'll turn up. You don't think its possible you have another nut running around out there, do you?"

Dane laughed before hanging up, "That's a play on words if I ever heard one. But no, I'm sure she'll turn up."

Kay and Donna joined Dane at his table for dinner that night putting their trays of franks and beans down next to his. "Not much of a choice, although I guess we're lucky to have anything hot."

Kay nodded, "I'm so hungry, I could eat a horse."

Donna nodded agreement, "Has anybody seen anything of the Kiernan girl yet?"

Dane sat up in shock, "No, damn it. I've been so busy that I forgot about her. I also forgot to call Sgt. Nugent. Dicks said he was going to have him assigned to us until they can clear the roads." He finished his coffee and hurriedly went to the command post.

⇒ Chapter 29

Drack watched Belial move to the wall containing the shelves of mason jars with his trophies. He placed the breasts and vagina from the Kiernan girl into a mason jar. He filled the jar with embalming fluid and put it on the shelf with the rest of his collection. Later that night they would take her remains and bury it in the snow as far from the hospital as possible. By the time the snow thawed he would be long gone.

The blizzard upset his plans to begin his retirement from the hospital. The trapped feeling and weariness from the overwork sent wall after wall of his mind crashing and Belial was in control excepting when making his rounds. Even then, Drack would have flashbacks and Belial would begin whispering. Most of the pictures were of his mother, her flaxen hair and huge breasts moving under the embraces of his uncle and the bearded stranger. The urge to kill were stronger and incessant.

The blizzard raged on, blocking all side roads and feeder highways. Highway maintenance crews fought valiantly to clear the snow from expressways but only managed to keep one lane open each way on the Long Island Expressway and Southern State Parkway. The radio kept announcing the location of emergency shelters and urging people to seek shelter in them. The storm, stalled by high winds settled over Long Island and continued to dump snow on the hapless Island.

Winds, which at times reached a hundred miles an hour, created drifts up to thirty feet in areas, sometimes burying entire houses. Power poles that were not knocked down by the winds had their lines snapped by fallen trees or flying debris. Locations that had a source of stand by power such as hospitals, schools and police stations were filled to capacity with people seeking shelter. Queens Park was no exception and one of the last to struggle in was the big sergeant, Pat Nugent.

By chance Donna was in the lobby when he walked in and she flew into his arms.

Dane was in the command post when Nugent came in, "My God, am I glad to see you."

"I was going crazy in the house. I only live three blocks from here, but it took the better part of an hour to get in."

"What about your family?"

"The kids are grown up and gone from the house over two years. The wife is a nurse at St. Charles and has been there since the storm began," he shrugged, "We haven't gotten along for quite awhile and we're pretty close to a divorce."

"Let me fill you in on our situation. We only have about a third of our normal staff and only sixteen of our male aides."

"What about your security people?"

"Just two of them and they are afraid to go into the violent wards. None of the men who live close by have volunteered to try to make it in. I can't blame them. For seven bucks an hour, you don't get heroes. At any rate, we have plenty of food, even though most of it is hamburger or franks and beans. We have our own power station and plenty of fuel to keep it running, so we have light and heat. Our biggest problem is security, Dane frowned, "One of our young nurse's aides is missing."

Nugent stared at Dane, "You don't think you've got another killer on the loose?"

"Not really. In fact, the last conversations I had with Dicks before the phones went dead again, he felt that the odds were a million to one we had another one. But she hasn't shown up for two days and she lives too far from here to have tried to go home."

Nugent stood up, "Let me meet your with male aides and I'll pick a squad for security detail and organize a search party and set up watches for the night. We can have the men operate in pairs and be on daytime patrol. Meanwhile send a warning out that no one is to go anywhere alone, day or night."

"We have accomplished one thing. We've found a map of a set of tunnels that link all the buildings together and have established contact with the other wards."

"No kidding? What kind of tunnels?"

Dane gave the Sergeant a copy of the map and explained the lighting system they had set up and the contacts with the other wards.

Nugent grasped the map and said, "I'm impressed. You've done a hell of a job organizing."

Kay came in as Nugent was leaving, "Donna is waiting for you in the cafeteria. She says you owe her a cup of coffee."

Before he left, one of the doctors came in and announced that they found the Professor dead in his bed.

Kay began crying, "That gentle man. What happened to him?"

"It looks like a heart attack but we won't be sure until we can do an autopsy." The doctor looked out the window at the snow piling up on the sill, "and that isn't going to take place until this storm lets up and we can get some help."

Dane put his arms around Kay, "The man has been ill off and on. It sounds as though he didn't suffer."

⇒ Chapter 30

Drack paced from one wall to another in his collection room. He once again was increasing his reliance on Prozac and cocaine. He needed the drugs in order to continue with his hospital duties. Because everyone was wearing down with the work and lack of sleep, no one seemed to notice his shambling gait or slurred speech. Belial was growing more insistent in his urging him to kill. It no longer mattered whether the next victim was either male or female, young or old. One night he came upon the alcoholic Dr. Paul sleeping in a stairwell and killed him on the spot.

Now another voice joined with Belial urging him to kill. This time the voice was that of a female. The voice was vaguely familiar. The two of them were screaming that he had to dispose of Popeye. But how?

Dane sat next to Kay at breakfast, toying with the powdered eggs and spam, "Lets go over to the station. I haven't been alone with you since you came in."

Kay grinned salaciously, "I thought you'd never ask."

"I'll get a map and a flashlight and meet you around ten. Ask Donna to cover for you. Give her the station's number in case any one is looking for me."

Glad to escape from the noise of the cafeteria and with a tingling sensation in her groin, Kay made her way to the medical room that was set up by the doctors to handle any emergency calls. Donna was there in deep conversation with Nugent. She turned as an aide handed her a memo, "Son of a bitch!"

As the aide was approaching Kay, she asked Donna, "What's wrong?"

"That asshole. Liebman has scheduled a team meeting for this morning."

Kay was furious, "A meeting? We don't have time to sleep and he's called a meeting?"

Donna said, "I hear it's about Popeye. He and one of his buddies got into some medicinal alcohol and mixed it with some cans of soda. They got loaded and Popeye tried to hang himself. His buddy, Kenna got violent and they had to put them both in sheet restraints. One of Popeye's treatment team is insisting on a meeting."

⇒ Chapter 31

Drack was half asleep as the monthly treatment meeting started. The nights without sleep and the accumulation of drugs in his system was beginning to take its toll.

No one noticed that his condition was deteriorating because everyone in the hospital was overworked and on edge. Complaints had been made before the blizzard hit to the union as more violent patients were being transferred from upstate mental institutions and the staff was not being increased. The union as usual did nothing but hold meetings.

Dr. Liebman was droning on endlessly outlining the format of this months meeting. Several of the Doctors challenged the idea of the meeting, protesting that they were stretched to the limit because of the shortage of help. Two arose and silently walked out.

Liebman flushed, "We are only going to work on the most serious of cases. In particular, those who are feeling the effects of our isolation. I specifically want to discuss Jack Cataldo, whom you all know as Popeye."

Drack snapped to attention as he heard Dr. Liebman mention Popeye, "This patient, an Italian American, Jack Cataldo, known as Popeye, has recently regressed to complaining of hearing

**command voices telling him to hurt himself. He also is fearful that
an unnamed member of the staff is going to kill him."**

A murmur from the assemblage caused the Doctor to look up
from his notes, "Please pay attention, I know how well you all like
Popeye but we have four other patients who are deteriorating as badly
as Mr. Cataldo. These five patients were responding well to chemical
treatment until this storm hit. But the five of them are steadily getting
worse. We therefore feel that the only way, short of sheet restraint is set
up a one day procedure for ECT for the day after tomorrow."

Dr. Abbott stood, his face flushed with anger, "I want to go on
record as being opposed to this treatment. There is still too much that
we don't know about shock treatment."

Farkis also stood, "Nonsense, it has been proven as a treatment for
years now."

"It is an inexact science. For Christ's sake, we don't know what's
going on in ninety percent of the brain and you want to deliberately
cause a seizure in an already brain disabled patient."

Doctors were standing all over the room, most supporting the
treatment, "We are not in the dark ages anymore. ECT has been
proven effective in bring schizophrenics out of their depression and it's
a simple procedure."

Dr. Liebman held his arms up to stop the argument, "Hold it down!
We can't get anything done with people shouting at each other. Dr.
Farkis will present a report from the New England School of Medicine
which supports our decision to conduct this procedure."

The square grey woman stood, her baritone voice overriding the
swirls of discussion still emanating from the assemblage, read from
the report, "Electroconvulsive therapy has been proven as a safe and
significant method of treating certain types of schizophrenia, depression

and mania. Most treatment centers will not give ECT until the patients have tried psychotherapy and antidepressants. In the fifties it was much abused with patients getting as much as three times a day."

She halted her report as a young Filipino doctor interrupted, "We know so little of the effect on any mind when jolted with electricity. I've read these reports but what they don't mention is the patients who are severely burned and sometimes die."

Another Doctor answered without rising, "We've been doing these treatments for two months and have had nothing but success. Their medical histories are studied to be certain there is no physical possibility of harm. When we put them through the ECT, we closely monitor them with EEG and EKGs."

Dr. Abbott rose, "I have a copy of a report I'd like to introduce------."

Dr Liebman spoke out, "Please! Let Dr. Farkis finish her report and then we'll listen to your objections."

Dr. Farkis glared at Abbott and continued, "The report further states that there were only 45,000 patients treated last year with but just a few bad reactions."

"Who says? Only a few states track how many people are treated with ECT. Last year California, one of the few tracking it reported almost 3,000 cases. Extrapolate that and you get over 100,000. You don't mention the headaches and the severe loss of memory in many of the patients. I grant you that patients are helped with the treatment but no one knows about the long term damage. I'm for stopping the usage until we get more facts."

Liebman pleaded with his audience wherein a shouting match erupted between the doctors, "Please, stop shouting. We will do these few and I promise to put a halt to any other treatments until we get a further report. Besides, we already have the permits signed by the patients and it will make it easier to handle the patients."

A voice from the gathering spoke up, "That doesn't say much. Most of these people would agree to a brain transplant without anesthesia if you asked them."

Laughter broke the tension, but they became quiet when Dr. Abbot said as he strode out of the meeting, "You're going to turn these people into vegetables just to make it easier to handle them."

Dr. Liebman pleaded with the remaining staff, "Popeye, Kenna and the other three patients have become a danger to you people as well as themselves. We don't have the necessary staff to handle them. We are going to give them the procedure as stated."

Dr. Farkis sat quietly through the rest of the meeting with a slight smile of triumph.

➣ Chapter 32

The snow stopped falling on the belabored island and road crews aided by the National Guard were able to partially clear some of the main highways. Phone lines were repaired and some communication was established. Huge army 4 x 4 trucks were used to plow through to some houses to rescue ill and elderly patients and bring them to local hospitals.

Drack stumbled through the catacombs, choking on occasion from the foul odor in the tunnels. The breathing vents situated over the tunnels were blocked by seven feet of snow. Belial, his voice daily becoming louder in Drack's head ordered, "We'll now have that piece of shit Popeye in our hands. We'll slip into the treatment room tonight and increase the jolt that thing puts out."

Sensing the doubt Drack felt, the familiar female voice cackled, "You'll do fine. You're a reader, remember? Read on how to do it!"

Dane and Kay were in the hospital entrance when the first heavy army trucks pulled up. The soldiers began emptying the truck of its human cargo.

One of the aides protested, "You'll have to take them to one of the regular hospitals, we're not set up for medical aid."

188

The soldiers kept emptying the trucks while a beefy Sergeant answered, "These people need help and you're the closest thing to a medical facility we have close enough."

Doctors rushed to the site as the patients, mostly elderly were laid on the floor. A makeshift emergency room was quickly set up in a portion of the cafeteria. Two elderly ladies who were unconscious were put into a small room off the cafeteria and two doctors immediately began treatment to revive them.

Dane asked Kay, "What's their problem?"

Kay who was busy trying to get information from the conscious people said, "They're two sisters who were trying to keep warm in their house with a charcoal burner. Neighbors who were at the high school didn't find them among the people who made it there. When the storm broke the police and National Guard began questioning people as to any missing persons. The Guardsmen broke into the sisters' house and found them unconscious. They're in pretty bad shape."

Donna came in as they were talking, "I've been assigned to one of the shifts to take care of them. There isn't much we can do except putting them on oxygen. We have another problem, those guardsmen brought in a woman that looks as though she's going to pop any minute. We sure as hell are not equipped to handle a newborn."

Nugent came in as the three were talking, "I hate to tell you this but the other storm the weatherman was warning us about is going to hit us tonight."

Kay was aghast, "My God! I've got to check with my sister to see how they are situated as far as food and heat."

Dane said, "See if they can get to a shelter during this lull," turning to Nugent, " we'd better check our food supplies and oil. With all the extra people and this new storm coming in we could be in for a long siege."

The new storm was another slow moving mass that settled over Long Island and began dropping snowflakes as large as a mans hand. Heavy winds began to build with some gusts up over sixty miles an hour. The few telephone lines the repairmen had put back up were quickly felled. Trees were going down all over the Island blocking the few side streets that had opened. Motorists were being found frozen to death in their snow covered cars. The radio reported that an estimated three thousand people were unaccounted for. Each home and emergency shelter was an oasis in a white desert.

→ Chapter 33

Drack silently entered the cafeteria and navigated past the cots that were set up in the corner for the refugees that were brought in today. Belial was taking over more and more of his conscious thought and was contemplating slaying some of the figures on the cots or perhaps the blonde nurse hovering over the two small figures in the room off the cafeteria. The nurse Donna looked up from the book she was reading, smiled and waved at him. He considered taking her but reluctantly passed with a wave. There were too many potential witnesses who might awaken and catch him. Besides, tonight was the opportune time to shut up Popeye.

He paused at the door of the ECT lab, looked around, seeing no one opened the door with his pass key.

Swiftly moving to the long table at the center of the room, he went to the head of the table where the ECT machine was. The box, looking like a stereo speaker had wires leading from it attached to two electrodes hanging from the box. Bending over the equipment, he unscrewed the plate over the voltage meter and tightened the needle indicating voltage. Taking a small alligator clip he ran a small thin wire to the plug leading to the ground wire. The wire, almost invisible, would triple the amount of voltage coming from the outlet. Giggling, he replaced the plate and silently left the room.

Popeye sat nervously in the waiting room with two other patients as a woman was led into the ECT room. He didn't raise his head to peer through the door. He had been given a mild barbiturate which normally would relax him. It didn't seem to take effect and his feet began to nervously tap the floor. The other two patients, Kenna and another man, were in a similar state. The only other occupants of the waiting room were two burly aides, both looking bored and flipping through old magazines.

The silence was broken by screaming coming from the treatment room. The three patients rose to their feet and bolted for the exit. The startled aides intercepted them and forced them to return to their seats.

The screaming stopped as quickly as it began, Dr. Liebman came out and apologized, "She isn't hurt. She awoke and became frightened. She will be coming out in a few minutes."

The doctor went back into the room and the three frightened patients looked at each other and quickly stared at the floor. About ten minutes passed and a doctor led the woman out. She looked dazed but was speaking coherently to the doctor as she and a nurse left the room.

Soon they come out for Popeye and he was led trembling into a brightly lit room where several doctors are setting up the table for him. Obediently, he took off his shoes and socks and laid down on the table.

One of the doctors read from Popeye's folder, "Doctor Liebman, all of the forms are present and signed including the declaration by the patient's psychiatrist of the patient's competency to understand this procedure and its possible side effects. Ah damn it, the Associate Medical Director is supposed to countersign the damned form next to the ward doctor's declaration of competency. We'll have to cancel the procedure."

Dr. Liebman grabbed the file and read it, "Popeye has signed the form and everything else is in place. I'm not going to go all through this. I'll sign the damned thing. Taking a pen from his jacket, he hastily signed the statement and said, "Lets get this over with."

The other personnel in the room stared at one another, one of them said, "I want to go on record that I'm opposed to going on with this until the Associate Medical Director of the Patients Rights has signed this."

Dr. Liebman waved the doctor out of the room and leaned over Popeye, saying in a pleasant monotone, "Don't be frightened Popeye. I'm going to explain everything we are going to do and how you will feel when it is finished, "picking up a pair of electrodes, "we are going to wash your head with alcohol and then place these, on the left side of your head. We then hook you up to these (pointing to the EEG and EKG equipment) so we can monitor you while the treatment is going on. Do you understand?"

Popeye nodded yes, although he hadn't heard a word the doctor said. He was too busy watching fearfully as a nurse hooked him up to an intravenous tube which was feeding him barbiturates and a muscle relaxer. The aide then put a bite-block in his mouth and Dr. Liebman turned on the machine. The monitor reading on Popeye's pulse rate read 75 and brain waves and oxygen levels were normal. Saliva began to ooze from the left side of his mouth.

One of the orderlies who was monitoring the EEG said with a worried frown, "Doctor, his pulse rate just shot up to 150."

DR. Liebman said calmly, "That's within normal parameters. His EKG is normal. We only have fifteen seconds to go."

The pulse rate advanced higher with astonishing speed. Popeye' toes curled and his body became rigid with tension. Smoke began to curl up from the electrodes attached to his head. Dr. Liebman blanched and one of the attending doctors immediately switched off the unit. A total of fifteen seconds elapsed. Popeye's brain had literally been fried.

In the consternation and horror surrounding Popeye and his accident, no one noticed one of the doctors leaving the treatment room.

⇒ Chapter 34

Drack hurried back to the cafeteria, Belial laughing so loud that Drack placed his hands over his ears to soften the sound. "We've done it. There are no witnesses left. As soon as the way is clear we'll leave this dung heap."

The woman's voice suddenly said, "While we are waiting we can still try and kill the bitch."

An angry Dr. Abbott stormed into the command post where Dane and Nugent were laying out the schedule for the teams, "Jim, you've got to exert some influence on that simple bastard, Liebman."

"Why? What's he done?"

"I begged him to hold off the shock treatments on the patients and now he's half killed Popeye."

Nugent laughed, "Shock treatments? I thought that stuff went out about the time the Frankenstein movie was made."

Abbott glared at Nugent, "It's not funny. There was something wrong with the machine and Popeye is still unconscious. We have no idea how much brain damage he suffered or if he is even going to awaken."

Dane said, "Jim didn't mean anything. He doesn't see your patients in the same light as you doctors."

"That's the trouble with people. These folks are stored away like winter clothing and forgotten by the public until one of them makes a juicy headline like Olsen."

Kay walked in with a troubled look, "I heard about Popeye. My God, aren't we ever going to go back to normal?"

Before Dane could answer, the phone rang and he picked it up. It was one of the orderlies in the ECT room. He asked Jim to come right down. It was obvious that someone had tampered with the ECT machine.

———————

Kay insisted on going to the lab with Dane and Nugent. As they entered the anteroom, Liebman and the therapist, Dr. Farkis followed them. The orderly, who had placed the phone call to Dane was still in the room waiting for them, "Here's the problem, Mr. Dane. Someone put an alligator clip and another wire onto the ground. It acted as a boost to the current being fed to the head clamps."

Dr. Liebman, wringing his hands, "Then why didn't the gage show the increase? It didn't go over 100 volts."

The orderly pried the glass covering up from the face of the gage, "Someone tightened the screw on the indicator. You may have been giving him anywhere from 200 to 400 jolts of electricity."

Liebman threw up his hands and stepped backward, "I don't believe it. There has to be some sort of malfunction in the equipment."

Nugent who had been examining the machine, arose shaking his head, "There's no mistake. The faceplate has been tampered with and there is an extra wire attached to the plug. It runs to the 220 out let in the wall." He bent over the unit, "There's a switch on the back indicating that you can run this on either 110 or 220. The switch is set at 220."

The aide who operated the unit said, "That's impossible. We've used this equipment hundreds of times and it's always set at 110 and plugged into the 110 outlet. That switch is set up by the Japanese manufacturer. They always have a switch like that on all their electronic equipment. That way they can sell it all over the world and into those countries that are still on 220."

Kay with a tremor in her voice, said, "My God! Who would want to hurt such a nice man? Why?"

Dane and Nugent stared at each other. It was Dane who answered her question, "It may well be that Olsen wasn't acting alone." He stared at the equipment, "Or, since this has to be someone with a knowledge of the machine, it could be one of the staff."

"And that means we and five thousand souls are trapped here with a homicidal maniac and cut off from any outside help."

→ Chapter 35

Drack sat at the chair at a desk outside the conference room watching the meeting in the command post. Present was the hospital police chief, the county trooper, the bitch and several of the lead Doctors and therapy aides. Drack was invited to the meeting but begged off as being too busy. He avoided as much direct contact with the staff as possible. He felt small pieces of his mind caving in and voices constantly talking to him. He was dosing himself heavily with Prozac in order to function and when he found that the drug was leaving him too much in a zombie like trance he would give himself a dose of heroin to give him the lift he needed to interact with people. The voices were now continuously urging him to kill. Their recklessness was somewhat offset by the drugs. On several occasions, Belial would disappear and the woman's voice was became stronger. When she was paramount, he began to kill men as well as woman, old as well as young. On one of his trips past the command post he paused to listen to the meeting while leaning casually against the door jamb. His eyes couldn't leave the bitch although from time to time his attention would shift as one of the members mentioned something applicable to him. He stiffened as he heard of the suspicions that another serial killer was loose. He straightened and left the doorway in a panic when it was decided to form search groups to examine the tunnels more thoroughly.

The storm clung to Long Island like a malevolent spirit, blowing freezing death to people of the island and road clogging drifts to its roads. The governor designated the island a disaster area and mobilized the National Guard again. It was a pathetic gesture meant more as a political move more for the voters than an effective rescue effort.

Few of the militia were able to answer the call to get to the station houses. What few who could straggle in were helpless. The Guard was unable to move their heavy equipment more than a few feet from their headquarters. Howling winds of one hundred miles an hour was blowing stretches of the highways on the South Shore clean of snow but leaving treacherous areas of impassable black ice.

The bridges and tunnels from Manhattan were passable at times but any traffic attempting to enter Brooklyn or Long Island City were met with white chaos. The ferry service from Connecticut to the island was halted at the beginning of the storm when one of the ferries almost foundered leaving New Britain. The only communication with the outside world was the pockets of population that had back up power supply units. Some enterprising home owners brought their car batteries into their homes and attached them to their television sets. Other homes relied on portable radios for news and passed the information on to their neighbors. Those homes with gas heat were able to keep fairly warm and became havens for their neighbors. A huge metropolitan area regressed back into medieval conditions. Nature began killing people by the thousands.

Dane opened the morning meeting, "We're completely on our own and can't expect help for days, maybe weeks. Fortunately, we have enough food and fuel for a month and we have medical personnel and facilities to take care of any health emergency. Dr. Abbot found an old handbook that was put out by the state back in the fifties that covered an emergency in case of an atomic attack." He grinned in response to a smattering of laughter from the group. "It's almost the same thing if you want to look at how isolated we are."

Dr. Liebman said, "Isn't there any way we can get our strongest men to go out and seek help?"

Nugent gave the doctor a withering glance, "Where would you like them to go, for Christ's sake? Two days ago the National Guard was bringing people to us for shelter. We have to make our plans to survive this thing and frankly, the first thing is to find out where the hell some of our people are disappearing to."

A frightened hush fell over the assemblage. Dr. Younger asked, "Who's missing now? The only ones I heard of were Dr. Paul and the Kiernan girl."

Dane answered, "We're so spread out that it's hard to keep track of all our personnel, much less five thousand patients." He spread out a map of the institution on the conference table, "My plan is to close the newer buildings and concentrate our patients in the older buildings from # 1 through # 10."

Dr. Abbott interjected, "Why close the newer and more efficient buildings? They also happen to be closest to the main highway where help is sure to come."

"Because, we are having a hell of a time getting to these buildings to take care of the patients. With the older buildings we can travel from building to building by using the underground tunnels. And forget about help from the outside. We're it."

One of the aides assigned to the violent ward asked, "What do we do with my patients? We can't mix them in with the regulars, we'll have a slaughter on our hands."

"I thought of that. We'll transfer them into Building 7 and place permanent guards at both sides of the tunnel leading to the entrance. We'll use some of my security people and arm them."

Donna looked anxious, "We never have allowed our security guards to be armed. Where will you get the guns?"

"There is a small weapons cache in the police section of the maintenance building. There are rifles and a few shotguns. I have six revolvers that we can arm our people with. Donna told me that there is a closet in murderers row that has a dozen tranquilizer guns. We'll pass those out as well. " Turning to Kay, "Can you get me a list from the database on personnel who have had some kind of military training?"

Kay nodded, "Do you really think it's necessary to have armed guards?"

Nugent broke in, "It's just a precaution and damned good sense to boot. Normally, if a crisis arose here, you could get help in less than ten minutes. We have a couple of hundred patients who have killed before and they have to be guarded around the clock. We simply don't have the necessary amount of aides to handle them on a personal basis to feed or medicate them. We're going to have to bring them to the cafeteria in groups of twenty to feed and medicate them."

Dane spoke up, "When we're through with one group we'll move them into building 10. It is the securest building on the grounds. Each floor is accessible through metal doors on each landing and the wards on each floor are broken into four self contained units. Each unit has its own bathroom facilities so that we don't ever have anyone enter a ward without an armed escort."

Dane looked up as he thought he heard a gasp and frowned, trying to remember who had been standing at the door, "The regular patients we'll herd into Buildings 1 through 5 with all the docile ones, such as the geriatric wards in Building 1."

The meeting broke up as each member with the exception of Dane and Nugent left to implement the plan.

Dane leaned back in his chair. He had a real mystery on his hands. A person or persons unknown were committing murders on his beat and he didn't have the huge resources of a modern police force to help him.

Kay broke into his reverie coming into the command post, bringing the print out of personnel who had military service or belonged to gun clubs. She gave each man a copy and while Dane and Nugent eagerly scanned it, Kay read the list aloud, "There are only a handful out of the seventy nine personnel still at the hospital with any kind of weapon training. Drs. Abbott, Younger, Paul, the six security people from the hospital force, and of course Sergeant Nugent and Lieutenant Dane and Donna Burns complete the list. There may be more but these were the only ones who filled out the hobby section of the personnel application with this data. You may want to canvas the rest of the personnel to see if anyone else has a background or knowledge of firearms."

Dane said, "We can discount Dr. Paul, he's either on a drunk or coming out of one. I'm surprised to see that Donna did a lot of hunting with her husband while he was alive and belonged to several gun clubs. That gives us a total army of eleven people."

Dane turned to Nugent, "Sergeant, I'm going to put you in charge of passing out the firearms." Turning to the rest of the assemblage, he said, "I'm placing Dr. Younger in charge of relocating the non-violent patients to building 1 and Dr. Abbott in charge of moving the violent patients to Building 2 and 3."

Dr. Liebman stood and pompously said, "Now see here, I'm still in charge of this institution. Nobody brought me into these plans."

Dane waved impatiently at the fat man, "We don't have time to argue with you. The sergeant and I worked this plan out last night. We're just trying to see that everybody gets through this storm alive."

Nugent gave the doctor an amused smile, "Doc, we have a job for you. Pick out two of the nurses, I suggest that Mrs. Burns be one of them and have her collect all of the drugs from each of the drug lockers in each of the buildings. We'll put them in a locked area here in the command post."

Donna Burns said, "That's an excellent idea. I also think we should collect all the keys that are floating around."

Nugent looked up from the plans, "What keys?"

Donna explained, "Each door leading into every building is locked and requires a pass key to get in. Each ward also has a steel door that automatically locks when it closes. Everyone on the wards has a special key to go from ward to ward."

Nugent swore, "Jesus! There has to be a million keys floating around."

Kay broke in, "Not really. Everyone is given a set of keys to enable them to move from building to building and ward to ward. We have to sign for these keys and use them several times a day to do our job. If you lose one, you have to report the loss to your supervisor and you are fined $100.00. If you lose it a second time, you are brought up before a committee and are subject to termination. The only keys that are here in the hospital at this time are with the personnel still on the grounds. The rest of them are home with the people who couldn't make it to work."

Dane said, "We really don't know who are killer or killers are or if they are a patient or someone from staff. If he or she has a key, we have a problem."

Chapter 36

Drack sat in his collection room, raging at the invasion of his catacombs by the teams moving patients to their new quarters. The voices of Belial and the woman were constantly at him to seek out and kill a straggler. Anyone. At times, Belial would take command of his body and Drack would find himself floating above as his body moved around. Other times, the woman's voice was stronger, sneering and mocking staff and patients.

Drack had to help in the process of moving the patients and was lucky enough to catch a pair of stragglers who had slipped away from the main body of patients. The man was a young patient who was due to be discharged but was trapped in the hospital by the blizzard.

Drack was hunting for stragglers when he came upon them, standing in a stairwell of one of the buildings, the female with her hospital gown up around her waist, the man just entering her, his arms braced against the wall to support him. Belial took the man first in a savage attack that nearly cut the man in two. As the man fell, he grabbed the woman by the throat and slammed her repeatedly against the wall, certain she was unconscious. He was startled when she grabbed his knife hand and began struggling with him. She was incredibly strong and he began to feel fear as she gripped his knife hand and began fighting back. She was a square, bulky woman who really belonged in the violent ward but had been mistakenly grouped with the geriatric group.

Using his knife hand she spun him into the stairs. The impact caused him to drop his knife. He was disconcerted, when instead of fleeing, she attacked, growling and cursing. She grabbed him by the throat and began strangling him. Fear and anger gave him extra strength and he fought her off, trying to reach his knife.

As he bent down, the woman leaped on his back, howling all the while with maniacal screams. She had powerful hand strength and was twisting his head in an attempt to break his neck. Drack was finally able to grab the knife and in a series of backward thrusts into the side of the woman, her hold on him began to loosen. When she finally fell to the ground, Drack slashed her throat and staggered into the catacombs and ran to the entrance to his home. It was the first time he had slain a woman without taking a trophy.

Nugent led an obviously upset Dr. Abbott into Dane's office in the command post. He told the staff in the room without a preamble, "Dr. Abbott just told me that he is missing two people from a group that they were transferring from Geriatrics to Building One."

Abbott said, "We didn't realize that anyone was missing until we counted heads when we were assigning beds."

Dane said hopefully, "Maybe they got lost in one of the turns and will show up later."

Abbott shook his head, "We retraced the tunnel clear back to Geriatrics and found no trace of them."

"Do you know their names?"

"He's Kevin Hansen, a revolving door patient with a history of alcohol and drug abuse. He was actually discharged and referred for outpatient services."

"Is he violent?"

Abbott nodded, "He can be, but the woman he's with is extremely dangerous."

"Then, what the hell is she doing with Geriatrics? Don't you try to keep the older, docile ones separate from the rest of the hospital population?"

Abbott nodded and said in a defensive tone, "It was a mistake made by one of the new nurses. We're all tired and overworked. Some of these kids are doing jobs that they're not trained for." Abbott leaned over Kay and typed in the woman's name. "I want you to see what we're dealing with."

The computer screen came up with the report:

Form 142 MED	PSYCHIATRIC ASSESSMENT	State of New York Office of Mental Health

PSYCHIATRIC ASSESSMENT	Patients Name Roberta French	Aliases AKA Frenchy,

Sex:	Evaluation Date Female	7/28/88

	Admission Date 7/26/88	D.O.B: 6/29/47

	Facility Name: Queens Park Psychiatric	Unit/Ward No 22/219

Dane scrolled down past the personal data to get to the woman's history.

1. History of emotional and Behavioral Problems:

Patient is a 41 year old white, Catholic, single female who was transferred to QPPC on a 8.39 status. She was sent to this facility from Mid-Hudson Psychiatric when it was in the process of closing. Apparently in recent weeks her mental status has deteriorated and she has exhibited agitated and inappropriate behavior such as urinating in bed as well as on the floors of her residence. She has also exhibited threatening behavior, throwing furniture at other patients and became verbally abusive and threatening to this writer. When two aids attempted to calm her, she displayed enormous strength by ripping a metal chair from its floor fastenings to use as a weapon.

2. She is sexually active and killed her last partner by breaking his neck. She is considered extremely dangerous and is not to be allowed the freedom of the grounds unless escorted by two aides.

Dane looked up from the screen, "Jesus Christ! How long was she in with the old folks?"

"Just a day or so. She got mixed up with them when we started moving people."

Dane shook his head in amazement and turned off the computer, "How dangerous is this Hansen?"

Abbott shook his head, " As I said before he could be a problem when drinking. He's an airhead that scrambled his brains with coke and booze. The only real danger is a propensity for suicide. I wouldn't be surprised if we find that she's killed him."

Dane looked up at Nugent, "She could be the answer to our recent problems."

"Do you think she's responsible for our missing people?" I'm talking about Dr. Paul and the Kiernan girl."

Dane thought for a moment, "She sure as hell fits the bill", turning to Abbott, "Do you know if she had the freedom to commit any attacks on our people?"

Abbott frowned and threw up his hands, "God knows. With the few people we have handling so many patients, anything is possible."

Nugent said, "We had better organize an armed search party and check out the entire tunnel system and the empty buildings. We'll start out from the furthest building out and work our way back to here. That way, the only way she can run is back here and into one of our teams."

Dane nodded and began planning the make up of the search parties.

➤ *Chapter 37*

Drack cleaned the blood from his hands and face as a result of the fight with the woman, still shaking from the terrible struggle. The bloody clothes he discarded and put on a clean uniform. Dosing himself with Prozac, he went out into the tunnel and made his way back to the command post. As he entered the main building, he heard his name being called along with many others to join the group at the command post.

Dane checked the groups before they headed out to be certain that each group had a walkie-talkie and were well armed. He and Nugent planned to be at the command post, ready to respond to any call for aid from the groups.

Dr. Abbott led the first team out, going down into the tunnels with two burly aides. Donna Burns and an armed doctor brought up the rear. Their itinerary was to start from the left of the command post in the main building and work their way to the bottom of Building 7 and meet up with Team 2.

Team 2 was led by Dr. Younger, two armed aides and Dr. Farkis armed with a shotgun following. It had come as a surprise when she volunteered the information that she learned to fire a shotgun as a child. Dr. Younger's group's task was to enter the tunnel and begin searching the buildings from the Police and Fire Stations and continue until he reached the Citadel.

Dane and Nugent, armed with their pistols and two of the aides carrying rifles stayed in the command post. The patients and staff were curious and alarmed at the sight of so much weaponry and began to ask questions. Dane sent the pompous Dr. Liebman in to calm them and was surprised to find that he did an effective job.

The walkie-talkies began to squawk as the groups entered their first buildings and started searching.

Dr. Younger was the first to report, since he only had to go a hundred feet until he came to the entrance of the Police and Fire station. His voice crackled over the speaker, "We've covered the building and no one is here.

We're locking the doors behind us as we cover the rooms. The only strange thing we found is evidence that a bed has been put up in the police station and indications are that it's been used."

Kay heard the last as she entered the command post and blushed. Dane grinned into the mike and said, "I used it occasionally when I was forced to stay over."

Nugent saw the blush and the answering grin and smiled to himself. He had been looking for a place where he and Donna could tryst.

It was a full twenty minutes before Abbott reported in. "Jim, we're entering Building one. As you know, we have patients on the wards here and the place is loaded with people since we moved the geriatrics. The guards on the doors says that they haven't seen Frenchy. Any sense in going upstairs?"

Dane thought for a moment, "No, but search the stairwells and stairways on every building and be sure that each door is locked as you leave."

Nugent left the room and Dane turned to Kay, "Did you catch the grin on his face when Abbott mentioned the bed? He caught your blush. But, I can't believe he doesn't know about us, what with he and Donna being so close."

Kay smiled, "I guess I'm too old fashioned. Doesn't it bother you that other people know we're having an affair?"

He thought for a moment before answering, "Not really. It did in the beginning. Particularly when thoughts of Anna and the kids came to the surface."

She saw the look of pain filter across his face, "We never discuss Anna. In the beginning, after we made love, I know that you had feelings of guilt. That you were cheating on her."

He nodded, "We had that rare marriage of physical and mental love that became stronger through the years. Then, to lose her and the girls--------."

She saw the moistness in his eyes and felt a momentary pang of jealousy, "I understand or at least, I think I do."

"Don't you feel any sense of loss?"

She shook her head angrily, "No. Hatred, betrayal and outrage and the feeling for the first time in my life an urge to hurt someone."

She came to him and sat on his lap, holding his head and stroking his hair, when the walkie-talkie squawked, "Jim you and Nugent better come down here to Building 3. We've found Dr. Paul in the stairway. He's been butchered."

Jim told the aides who were in the hall outside the command post to man the radio and raced out to the door leading to the tunnels and ran into Nugent coming out of the cafeteria, "Let's go. They found Dr. Paul. He's been murdered."

The big sergeant gasped as they entered the tunnel, "My God! The air is getting worse down here."

Jim nodded, "We'll have to try to get a crew out to clear some of the air ducts closest to the buildings."

When Jim and the sergeant reached the entrance to building 3, most of the search crew were standing outside the door talking. One of the aides pointed silently to the door. Dane and Nugent entered and stood frozen for a moment stunned at the bloody scene. Dr. Younger was holding on to the metal banister, ashen faced while Dr. Farkis stood stoically, holding a shotgun across her chest as though on guard. The body of Dr Paul lay sprawled on the steps, his body cut almost in two by the savagery of the attack. His white uniform was dyed red with his blood. There were gaping wounds in his throat and chest.

Dr. Younger was hysterical, "I've never seen anything like this. Who could have done such a thing?"

Nugent answered without looking at the doctor, "It has to be those patients that disappeared from the group you were transferring. The woman has a hell of a past for violence."

Dane kneeled down by the corpse, "He was either passed out when he was attacked or he knew his killer."

Nugent asked, "How do you figure that?"

Dane pointed to Dr. Paul's hands, "There are no defensive wounds. It's natural for a victim to try to ward off an attack by putting your hands up against a knife thrust."

"We'd better get this bitch before she kills anyone else."

Dane nodded, "Don't forget that she isn't alone. That kid is apparently with her. He could be right up to his ass in the middle of this.

"I thought you told me that most serial killers are men. What's different here?"

Dane looked strangely at Nugent, "I didn't say that she's a serial killer, or that he is. Not with just one murder."

"What about the Kiernan girl? She hasn't shown up and she sure as hell isn't walking around outside."

Dane finished examining the body and stood, "This is the first body that we've gotten to while it was reasonably fresh. We'll have one of the MDs do an autopsy and see what he comes up with."

—————————————

Dane asked the medical doctors to volunteer to do an autopsy on Dr. Paul. Dr. Kenny, one of the more recent additions to the medical staff, raised his hand, "I'll give it a shot but we don't have any of the tools necessary for a professional job. I'm talking about high speed cameras and a proper table. I'm certainly not going to slice him up. We wouldn't be able to do an analysis if I did."

"All I'm looking for is anything that might tell us which one of these birds did the killing."

Chapter 38

Drack awoke feeling strangely refreshed and alert although having been asleep for only a few hours. Belial was now in complete control of all his actions. His body was just a shell in complete obedience to the voices of Belial, the woman and occasionally, Lew. He chuckled as he re-read the article in the Sunday supplement he brought home from the cafeteria. Drack never subscribed to newspapers and went to the hospital library for any reading he might wish to do. Even then, his reading was mostly limited to articles on mind altering drugs. The article he was presently reading was from one of Long Island's papers. The reporter wrote on the killings on the hospital grounds. The newspaper was almost three weeks old. There hadn't been a paper delivery to the hospital since the advent of the snow storms. The reporter zeroed in on the sensational aspect of the murders and referred to other serial killers such as Bundy, Gacy and others. Drack snickered as the reporter pointed out that most of the killers were abused as children and all had a career in crime. He wrote as though he was an expert in the field pointing out that these killers started out as burglars or peeping toms. Drack chortled with glee, if the police were as stupid as the reporter, then they would never catch him.

Dane and Nugent sat around the table in the command post reading the autopsy report on Dr. Paul. The doctor who volunteered to do the autopsy admitted that he really had never done any pathology but had observed some while an intern in a city hospital.

Dane read the report aloud to Nugent, "I don't have the proper forms for an autopsy but will tell you of my findings in the form that I can remember.

The body has been definitely identified as that of Dr. Abraham Paul, a white male, aged 38. The body is cold and rigor is present to an equal degree in all extremities. My final diagnosis is that he died of multiple stab wounds. The death blow being a deep wound in the chest to the left ventricle. The left 2nd , 3rd, 5th and 7th ribs are fractured due to the tremendous force of the stab wounds. The throat wound would have been sufficient for death were it not for the wound to the heart. The other wounds took place after death.

There was no evidence of head assault. That is, there was no sign of trauma to the skull. There was a huge amount of alcohol in the victim's urine specimen indicating that he was probably comatose when attacked. There was no evidence of any barbiturates, opiates or amphetamines in the victim's urine.

Lieutenant Dane's observation that there were no defense wounds is correct and the victim was apparently asleep when killed.

I close with the recommendation that the body be kept in our hospital morgue until the storm clears and it can be taken to the county morgue and a proper autopsy done by a qualified medical examiner."

signed,
Leonard P. Kenny M. D.

Nugent stood and said to Dane, "We'd better have the crews we organized start looking for those two birds before somebody else gets hurt."

"What worries me is the wounds described in the report are identical to those of some of the bodies we found after Olsen confessed."

"Jesus Jim, are you telling me that Olsen wasn't the killer?"

"No, he wouldn't know as many of the details of the killings as he did. But I'm afraid that it's beginning to look like Olsen had an accomplice." Dane eyed Nugent with a worried look, "there have been cases of serial killers working in pairs. Look at the case of those two cousins in California. They killed a bunch of girls and all the while the cops out there were searching for one guy." Dane tapped his fingers on the desk for a few moments, "Or we could have a copycat killer."

Nugent looked grim, "Lets feed the search parties and get them going again."

Dane nodded and began laying out the plans for the routes the search parties would take.

⇒ Chapter 39

Belial smiled as he fed Drack's body. The human was beginning to lose the ability to take care of the essential daily process of his body. The addition of the woman's voice supplanted that of Lew Thomas and was almost as strong as that of Belial. She was strident in her demands that they kill and pushed these demands to the point of recklessness.

Belial, however, was dominant and careful to bide his time in selecting his next victim. Meanwhile he would watch the bitch. He hadn't forgotten her. It was difficult to find her alone because of her duties and the fact that she seemed to always be in the company of the policeman. Belial kept watching them, knowing that sooner or later they would return to their love nest. The woman's voice was screaming louder that they should kill now. Just before the final wall of Drack's mind collapsed, he realized that the woman's voice he heard was that of his mother.

Dane called a meeting at the command post, "As you all know, Dr. Paul has been found. He has been brutally murdered," he paused, as a gasp arose from the few people assembled who hadn't learned of the death, "Sergeant Nugent and I are going to lead armed groups to try to locate two missing patients who might be responsible for the attack."

"What about the safety of the rest of us?"

"We are going to leave four armed men at both ends of the stairways. You can continue feeding and medicating the groups as we have been doing. But, and I can't emphasize how important this is, do not leave this section of the hospital without an armed escort."

Dr. Liebman spoke up, "There doesn't seem to be much doubt that Frenchy and Hansen are the killers."

Dane ignored the statement, "Dr. Liebman, I have an important job for you. I want you to pick out the strongest and most reliable patients and form them into snow shoveling details. We have to clear the breathing turrets around the buildings. The air in the tunnels is putrid."

Dr. Liebman raised his hands in protest, "I can't do that. State and Mental Health Department Rule prohibits us from forcing our patients to do manual labor."

Exasperated, Jim noticed the big black man, June Minney near the front of the group, "I've seen June sweeping the walks in front of some of the buildings in all kinds of weather."

Dr. Liebman smiled smugly, "He does this voluntarily. In his case, we feel that the exercise is excellent therapy. I can't and won't force him or anyone to shovel snow."

Dane stood and walked to the front of the crowd of patients, "Everyone who wants to shovel snow, raise your hands like this."

When Dane raised his arms over his head, all the patients, including elderly and infirm women, obediently raised their arms. Laughter erupted from the assembled staff who were joined by the patients. He glared at Liebman, "There, they all volunteered. I trust that you will see to it that they are all warmly dressed before they go out. You can take one crew and Dr. Younger can lead the others. Mrs. Teehan will be our co-coordinator at the command post."

Kay said, "I want to go with you. I don't have any experience doing this."

He led Kay back into the command post and away from the door where they had some privacy, "I want you to stay here where it's safe. And I do need someone to keep an eye on that old pussy and makes sure he gets those breathers cleared. The air down there is hell and we must use the tunnels if we're going to survive this."

He embraced her and she leaned into him, both were aroused at once. Kay felt an immediate warmth in her thighs and smiled, "When you come back, you are going to take me on a date to our nest."

Dane laughed and turned to leave, "It's a date."

As Dane and Nugent led their teams down into the tunnels, Kay and Donna went to the storeroom in back of the cafeteria where winter gear was kept. Several of the patients led by Minney followed them. They selected as much of the foul weather clothing they could find and went back to the cafeteria. They placed the clothing on a table and began putting the clothing on the patients who looked the fittest.

Dr. Liebman started to take a jacket back from one of the patients who began resisting him. As the struggle intensified, Donna angrily said, "Doctor, you're getting the men upset. You select the people who are going outside and Kay and I will hand out the clothing."

The doctor was choleric, "Mrs. Burns, I'm still head of this institution and I'll decide whom and when we'll send these people out into the storm."

Kay was furious and stepped in front of the man, "We have people in those tunnels searching for violent patients who have apparently killed. If Jim Dane says we have to clean the breathers around the buildings, then we're going out right now and begin shoveling. Either get dressed or get out of the way and let us do the job."

The doctor was stunned at the reaction of the two women, having never had his authority challenged by any of the nurses. He meekly stepped back as the patients began dressing. Kay was astonished but felt exhilarated at her outburst.

When twenty of the patients were fully clothed and as Kay was shrugging into her parka she said, "Dr. Kenny, please man the radio, I'm going out with Dr. Liebman. Lieutenant Dane and Sergeant Nugent will need someone to coordinate their search."

Dr. Younger and Donna was already leading their patients out the far entrance, the men excitedly talking, their shovels over their shoulders as though an army on a march. Kay led her group, followed closely by Minney.

She was stunned by the ferocity of the wind and freezing cold as she stepped out onto the pathway. Minney held the door open against the fierce wind and the patients obediently followed her to the first air hole. The breather was completely covered by a snow drift six feet high. Minney was the first to attack the drift and the rest of the patients followed his lead. They piled the snow around the breathers and patted it down with their shovels to make a temporary protection against the drifting snow. They were only able to clear two more before the cold and wind drove them back into the hospital.

Dr. Younger, Donna and their group were already back when Kay came into the cafeteria, "How did you guys make out?"

Kay gratefully accepted a cup of coffee from an aide, "We were able to do three of them before we were driven back. I don't know how long they'll keep them clear, though."

"We were able to do three as well, but we built a snow barricade around them so a couple of men going out every hour or so should be able to keep them clear."

Kay nodded, "As soon as we've warmed up we'll have to go into the tunnels and try the next building."

As Donna nodded agreement, Dr. Younger yelled out from the command post, "Lieutenant Dane says the air cleared up immediately and to keep up the good work."

Kay and Donna smiled and surprisingly, the patients cheered.

The snow crews, having been fed a hot meal were eager to go on to the next building. Three men inexplicably refused to go out into the cold again. Donna noted Kay's frustration, "Don't be upset. You never know what will turn a patient off from a project he's happy at. We're lucky it didn't set off a chain reaction among the other men."

Kay looked ruefully at the balking patients, "I understand that this happens, but it always surprises me."

"We have more than enough volunteers to make up for the loss."

As the snow crews were dressing, Dr. Younger contacted Dane and Nugent to alert them that they were going to be coming into the tunnels. He turned to Kay and Donna handing Kay the phone, "Dane wants to talk to you."

"Yes Jim."

"I want you and Donna to be careful coming into the tunnels. I'll send two of the search crew back to meet you at the stairwell at the bottom of the main building. Have Dr. Younger contact Nugent and have him do the same with Donna. You are not to move from the stairwell until the armed men reach you."

Irked at Dane's brusque command, Kay silently handed the phone back to Dr. Younger who set up the same arrangements for Donna's team.

Kay led her team down the stairs and stopped when they reached the stairwell leading to the tunnel. Kay defiantly opened the door and led her team into the tunnel. She was surprised to see Dane and the grim looking Dr. Farkis waiting for them, Dane gave Kay a hug, "I had a feeling that you were upset at my giving you orders like that, so I decided to come back and personally lead you to the next building."

"Where are the rest of your men?"

"Making sure that the next building is secure. It's slow work. They have to be sure the wards are all locked and then search the stairs, landing by landing."

"There shouldn't be a problem with these three buildings. They are all so close to one another and we have the geriatric patients housed there."

Dane nodded in agreement, and led the team in the direction of the complex containing buildings 1, 2 and 3, all the while holding Kay's hand.

Halfway to the complex, the phone crackled, it was Younger, "Jim this is Dr. Younger. The phone lines are up again and Lt. Dicks is on the line asking for you."

Kay saw Dane's hesitation, "Go on back. It may be important. At least you can tell them what's going on here."

Jim nodded, while glancing apprehensively at the huge black who had stopped and was gazing impassively back at them. Dane gave Kay his pistol, "I don't think you'll need this, not with the armed guards with the group. But please, stay close to the guards."

She nodded acquiescence and Dane raced back to the command post.

Dane took the stairs two at a time and raced down the hall to the command post and grabbed the phone proffered by Dr. Younger, "Hey Dicks, this is Jim."

"How are you guys doing?"

Dane felt relieved at being able to talk to the outside world, particularly the homicide detective, "We've still got trouble here. There are some patients missing and we have a couple of more murders on our hands."

Dicks was silent for a moment while he digested the news, "It's unheard of having two serial killers in the same area at the same time. Were the victims killed with the same M. O.?"

"No. It doesn't look like the same killer. One of the deaths is a man and Olsen only killed women, but it sure as hell is scaring the devil out of me. Any chance you can send some people here?"

"Sorry Jim. Every man that has been able to come in is out checking out of the way houses looking for storm victims. The only way we can travel is with National Guard trucks and we don't have a hell of a lot of them."

Dane sank wearily back into his chair, "Can they at least keep the lines up so we can let you know what's going on?"

"The telephone company has all the crews they can muster out working on the main trunks. Their problem is in keeping the lines up. The high winds are blowing branches across the wires and breaking them almost as fast as they put them back up."

Dane thought for a moment, "Can you at least look up some names for me on your computer?"

"Negative. We haven't been on line with the main frame for days. I can only check with what we have in our filing cabinets. What're the names?"

"I have a big black guy who makes me uneasy as hell, his name is June Minney. The others are Hansen and French. Can you look them up and get back to me?"

"I advise you to hang on while we search our filing cabinets on local people."

Dane said he would and a surprisingly short time later Dicks came back on the line, "We have some records on the Hansen kid. Nothing serious, just some drug busts. No history of violence. Zero on the other two. Don't you have a complete record on these people?"

"Yeah there's nothing definite on two of them but I'll bring up the screen on Minney. If there is anything else, I'll be in touch."

Dicks laughed, "Yeah, if the lines hold," and hung up.

Dane immediately began to scan the records on the computer looking for June Minney's hospital record. He felt a sense of unease after seeing the huge man in the tunnel with Kay. When he located Minney's records, he scrolled down past the admitting form and concentrated on the admitting doctor's notes.

SCREENING/ADMISSION NOTES   MINNEY, JUNE
                                 133597

DATE OF ADMISSION 09-11-62
                                 MALE   BLACK

LEGAL STATUS (INPATIENT)
INVOLUNTARY   DOB-03-26-42

1. SOURCE OF REFERRAL: PTS. SISTER CALLED POLICE.

2. REASON FOR REFERRAL/ADMISSION: THE PATIENT IS
A RETARDED MALE, OF STOCKY BUILD WITH LIMITED
EDUCATION. THREATENED TO KILL SISTER'S FIANCEE
WHEN HE ATTEMPTED TO MOVE IN WITH SISTER.
INJURED SEVERAL POLICE WHEN THEY RESPONDED TO
DOMESTIC COMPLAINT.

3. FAMILY COMPOSITION/LIVING ARRANGEMENTS:
LIVES WITH SISTER (ONLY KNOWN LIVING RELATIVE)

MOTHER DEAD, FATHER ABANDONED FAMILY WHEN
PATIENT WAS SIX. HIS PRESENT WHEREABOUTS
UNKNOWN.

4. PSYCHIATRIC AND OTHER SIGNIFICANT HISTORY
(INCLUDE CHEMICAL ABUSE): SEVERAL PSYCHIATRIC
ADMISSIONS, ELMIRA TWICE, QUEENS PARK TWICE. NO
KNOWN HISTORY OF SUBSTANENCE ABUSE. STRONG
MATERNAL FIXATION.

5. MEDICAL HISTORY, PHYSICAL CONDITION, CURRENT
DIAGNOSIS (INCLUDE NEUROLOGICAL DATA AND
CURRENT MEDICATIONS). ABNORMAL EEG IN ELMIRA
12/62. IN REMARKABLE PHYSICAL HEALTH DESPITE
BEING A HEAVY SMOKER. STARTED ON CECLOR FOR
CHRONIC BRONCHITIS.

6. MENTAL STATUS (INCLUDES ATTITUDE, BEHAVIOR,
MOOD, STRESS OF MENTAL ACTIVITY AND PRESENCE
OF DELUSIONS/HALLUCINATIONS) COOPERATIVE-
PSYCHOMOTOR ABNORMALALITIES. MOOD IS
TRANQUIL WHEN KEPT ACTIVE BUT BECOMES
DSYPHORIC WHEN CONSTRICTED. NO DELUSIONS OR
AUDITORY HALLUCINATIONS.

Dane leaned back in his chair and threw Minney's file on his desk. The file comforted him that the man was apparently no danger to Kay. It looked as though he had been struck by her kindness when she gave him the cigarettes. It also explained the man constantly sweeping and cleaning the steps in front of the hospital.

When the radio crackled to life, Dane was startled to hear Abbott's voice, "Jim, we've found our missing patients. They're dead. They've been murdered."

Dane yelled for one of the aides to man the radio and sped to the tunnel. As he ran, he noticed that some of the hurricane lamps were out and the tunnel was dark.

➤ *Chapter 40*

Belial watched and raged as the policeman and the bitch walked down the stairs to the tunnel. The pain of his wounds from the battle with the woman in the tunnel had not abated. None of the drugs he was feeding his body were helping and the order to centralize all drugs into one locker meant that his supply had to last him until he could leave. The pain only fueled his rage. His mother's voice was becoming more aggressive. She was constantly demanding more kills and reckless violence. It was also becoming increasing more difficult to find an opportunity to catch the bitch alone. His plans to have the host body leave the hospital would be completed as soon as the storm ceased. But first the bitch had to die.

The big sergeant led the way towards the maintenance building with Donna walking at his side. The air became foul again as they passed the last of the air holes that had been cleared. Nugent and the rest of the search team remained in the tunnel while the snow team was led upstairs to clear the air holes closer to the building. They passed Dane's office and smiled at each other upon seeing the bed.

Nugent held Donna back as the snow team went out into the storm and began clearing the area around the vents, "That bed room looks pretty inviting."

Donna pressed against Nugent and leaned hard into him, grabbing his head and giving him an open mouth, passionate kiss. She laughed as she felt him harden, "We can't do it now but why not come back here after wards?"

"I thought you'd never ask."

The patients came straggling back and Donna led them back to the main building while Nugent continued on to the old geriatric building.

Nugent led the way into the stairwell of the building and was the first to discover the bodies of Frenchy and Hansen. The bodies were sprawled at the bottom of the steps. He kneeled down and examined Hansen first. His face had a hideous death grin with an enormous slash in the throat. There was a deep wound to the abdomen, but the throat wound was the obvious cause of death. Nugent waved the other members of the search team back and ordered Abbott to call Dane.

Dane raced down into the tunnel and pushed past a milling group of patients and aides. He found Nugent standing over the bodies of Hansen and the woman. Nugent said, "She died the same way the kid did, with his throat cut. She also has series of knife wounds on her right side. She apparently put up a fight and hurt whoever it was, judging from the bruises on her hands."

Jim looked at the body of Hansen, "Could they have had a fight to the death?"

Nugent shook his head, "You're the homicide detective. But there isn't a knife anywhere and the kid must have died instantly and if you look at the marks in the dust, there was a hell of a struggle away from the boy's body."

"Then we've got another killer on our hands."

"Uh huh and it's not the same one. The woman hasn't been mutilated and you're the one who told me that these killers all have the same M. O."

"Do you know what the odds are that we have a second killer running around the same location?"

Nugent looked at Dane, "Out of sight, I guess, but we'd better get them back to our morgue and let Dr. Kenny have a look at them. That is, unless you want to leave them here until the storm lets up and we can get a forensics team in here."

"We can't do that. There's no telling when we can get anybody in here to help."

Dane had two of the aides go back to the main building for stretchers for the bodies. He examined the scene for something to point out the killer. The only items relating to the killer was the footprints and they were badly scuffed.

Dane returned to the command post, feeling sure he was overlooking something. He brightened when he saw Kay in the room alone.

She looked up as he entered the room, "Is this violence ever going to stop?"

He put his arms around her, "We're doing all we can to tighten up security. The patients are now all accounted for and everybody else is right here. We'll be alright until this damn storm passes."

She leaned into him, "I only feel safe when I'm with you."

Dane was amazed that in spite of the harrowing circumstances surrounding them that he could still be aroused, "I could stand a few hours away from here. Lets go to our place."

She smiled in agreement and only left his embrace when she heard someone coming into the room.

Chapter 41

Belial went into the room just in time to hear the bitch and her lover making plans for a tryst. It was difficult to hide his glee from the couple. The voice of his mother was howling with laughter at the promise of getting their hands on the bitch.

Belial hurriedly left the room before the couple and hastened to the stairs leading to the tunnel. He had to get to his home and get one of the surgical knives from his collection room. Belial no longer felt safe carrying one since security had been tightened. He put the rifle in one of the closets on his way to the stairwell. He considered using the weapon against the policeman but was confident that the element of surprise would eliminate the cop quickly. He would take him with the knife first and then bring the bitch to his collection room. He had to hurry because he wanted to get his weapon and then beat the couple to the room and be waiting for them.

Kay was about to head down the hall to meet Dane at the entrance to the tunnel when she heard her name called, "Mrs. Teehan, you have a phone call."

Kay hurried back to the command post and was handed the phone by an aide. As soon as she picked up the phone she recognized her sisters voice, "Hello Kay, I've been trying to get through to see how you're doing and to let you know that the kids are doing fine."

"We're in great shape here as far as food and warmth. We have our own heating plant and from what they tell me, plenty of oil. The diet is nothing to brag about but there's plenty of coffee and powered milk. What are you guys doing for food?"

"As you know we have gas heat, so we can cook and keep warm by the stove. We're kind of crowded now, we have neighbors who don't have heat camping out in the living room and the spare guest room."

Kay almost told her sister about the murders and kept silent figuring that there was no sense worrying them, "I really can't stay on the phone long. We're keeping the line open for emergency calls but let me say a quick hello to the kids."

"Believe it or not they're outside with the other kids supposedly trying to clear a pathway to the street. I think they've got about two feet open."

"O.K. tell them I love them and if I can get a chance, I'll call back when we don't have so many problems."

Kay put the phone down, suddenly missing the children terribly. She stared at the phone her eyes filling with tears, and shaking the depression, went to look for Dane.

Dane waited at the stairway and when Kay didn't meet him started back to look for her. As he passed the cafeteria, he was hailed by Dr. Kenny, "Mr. Dane, if you have a moment, I have something interesting to show you."

Dane hesitated for a moment and then followed Dr. Kenny to the room in back of the cafeteria where the temporary morgue was set up. The room was directly in back of the loading dock where deliveries were made. The area was partially open to the elements, and it was freezing cold, perfect as a temporary morgue.

Dr. Kenny picked up a steno pad from a table outside the actual morgue and read aloud from his notes, "This is a series of notes on a temporary autopsy done this day on a female patient, Roberta French, 5' 8" weighing approximately 170 pounds. Until a proper autopsy is done by a qualified medical examiner, I find that the cause of death was by a tremendous loss of blood from a slash wound in the throat from ear to ear. There are multiple stab wounds at the right 2nd, 3rd, and 5th ribs. The third and fifth rib are fractured indicating the force of the blows. The stab wounds are narrow at the top of the wound and jagged at the bottom indicating a knife with a serrated blade."

The doctor stopped reading and looked at Dane expectantly. Dane stared at the doctor, "So."

Dr. Kenny said slowly, "Remember, I'm no forensic expert but the stab wounds to the side reminded me of the stab wound in Dr. Paul. I checked again to be sure I'm right and they look pretty close to me."

"Then, it looks as though they were killed by the same person."

"I hate to tell you this Mr. Dane, but on a hunch, I examined the bodies of those three boys we found a week ago. The bodies are in pretty bad shape but the stab wounds look pretty consistent with the ones on Dr. Paul and this woman."

Dane stared at the doctor, "Jesus Christ. Then we have the same killer roaming the god damn hospital."

Dane immediately raced to the cafeteria and grabbed a bullhorn from the command post and barked, "Listen up everybody. It appears as though the serial killer who murdered those girls and the three boys in the tunnel is still with us. I want an immediate head count to see who is missing. I also want someone to take a count among the staff and then do the patients in the wards."

Dr. Liebman surprised Dane by reacting quickly by ordering two of the aides to check on the patients while he quickly did an attendance on the staff. He checked his list and told Dane, "Dr. Abbott, Dr. Farkis and Mrs. Tierney aren't here."

An aide at the back of the patients said, "I saw Mrs. Tierney by the stairway to the tunnel. She asked me if I saw you and I told her I thought you had gone down the stairs."

Dane told Younger, "Put armed guards at the each end of the cafeteria and don't let any body leave. Please have someone check the bathrooms to see if anybody is in there. Anyone coming from the tunnel is to be put under armed guard until I get back."

The aide closest to Dane turned to him looking puzzled, "Why?"

"Because you might be letting an insane killer in amongst you."

Dane, seeing the look of fear on the aide's face and satisfied that his precautions would be heeded, turned and raced toward the stairway leading to the tunnel. As he ran, he was filled with an icy dread of fear for Kay.

Kay arrived at the entrance to the stairway and not finding Dan, started down the stairs. She turned the flashlight on and fearfully opened the door to the tunnel. Not finding Dane, she was about to head back upstairs when the thought struck her that he might have gone on ahead looking for her. She shouted his name twice and didn't get an answer. Kay swept the flashlight up the tunnel and decided to go a little ways down. She stopped several times and shouted his name, to no avail. Kay was about to turn back when she spied the door to the maintenance room. She went to door and pulled it open and smiled. There was a faint light and the odor of kerosene coming from the stairs above. Dane must have gone ahead and lit the kerosene heater in order to warm the room for her.

Chapter 42

Belial raced down the darkened tunnel and arrived at his home just as the last hurricane lamp in the tunnel went out. He wrenched open the door from the tunnel to his collection room and felt along the wall until he found the big flashlight he kept next to the door. Flicking it on, he selected one of the surgical knives that he always kept as sharp as razors. He stopped momentarily, as he caught sight of the body of his last victim, still laying on the operating table. He never had the time to dispose of her remains. He would make room for the Teehan bitch when he brought her back.

He felt the heat rising as he glanced at the table in anticipation of having the bitch strapped to it as he worked on her. As he went out, he left the door to his home ajar so that when he came back with the woman, it would not be difficult getting back in again. Not wanting to take a chance on being seen in the tunnel with the flashlight, Belial kept it off until he arrived at the maintenance building. He flicked it on when he felt he was near the stairwell to the building and quickly found the door to the stairway. He went up the stairs to the first floor and opened the door, intending to find a spot to ambush the couple as soon as they entered the room. A small kerosene heater was on and gave off a feeble light, enabling him to find the door to the bedroom without turning on the flashlight. He was shocked to hear noise emanating from the *bedroom. The couple had somehow beaten him there. They must have left the command post at almost the same time he had. Belial hesitated momentarily, but the heat and lust for the kill was too great and he silently opened the door. The noises the couple were making were unmistakable and covered any sounds he made. He came within a few feet of the noises before turning the flashlight on. When he did, he held the knife high, intending to strike the cop on his back and then roll him off the woman and finish him on the floor with one stroke. The torch caught blond hair flailing in the light and shocked him for an instant. The woman had mounted the man on top and was turning toward him when he recovered. He struck her with a backhand blow and leaped to the bed and struck down with the knife. As he did so the man threw his arm up to ward off the blow but hit the flashlight instead. The flashlight went flying into the wall and flickered out. Belial plunged the knife into the cop's chest and was raising it to slash the man's throat when he was suddenly struck in the head, knocking him to his knees. The woman had recovered and was attacking him, using the heavy torch as a weapon. Her second blow caught him on his shoulder and he felt something break. He swung wildly with the knife and felt it strike home. The woman gasped and in a fury he grasped her by the hair and slashed furiously with the blade. A gush of blood told him he had hit a vital spot. The pain in his shoulder was agonizing, and he went to his knees to find the flashlight. Feeling along the woman's naked, motionless body he reached her hand and found the torch alongside of it. Getting shakily to his feet, he turned the light on in order to ascertain that the woman was dead, and if so, to claim his trophy. He heard a noise and turned the flash to the bed. The light barely caught the man and the gun he was holding, just as he fired. Belial felt a tearing, burning impact in his side that spun him into the wall. The cop fired again but this time the bullet went into the ceiling as he collapsed to the floor. Belial staggered to the door, dropping the knife so that he could hold the flashlight with one hand and his wound with the other. The taste of physical pain from his shoulder and side drove the kill lust from his mind. All that mattered now was to get back to his womb and heal his wounds. He cried out with pain as he put his arm up to brace himself against the wall of the tunnel as he staggered toward the door to his home. He was thankful that he had left the door ajar and was able to fit through the opening into his collection room. Laying the flashlight on the table, he lit the hurricane lamp and opened his medicine cabinet. Taking some amphetamine for the pain and to clear his head, he examined the gunshot wound. He took some gauze and cleaned the wound and was surprised that there was only a small hole in front but there was a larger hole where, fortunately, the bullet had exited. He cleaned the area with antiseptic and placed gauze pads over the wounds and wrapped a bandage around his waist to keep them in place. It was a slow, agonizing operation because of the pain in his left shoulder. Now that he had attended the bullet wound, he closely examined the shoulder. There was a small indentation where the woman struck him with the flashlight. He attempted to raise his arm over his head but had to halt with the arm at shoulder level. It was obvious that she had broken a bone in his shoulder but there was nothing he could do to heal it at the present time.*

Now that the bitch was dead, he would simply hole up in his lair until the storm ceased and he could get away. He raged that the woman was dead and he couldn't inflict the pain upon her. He would have given her moments of pain and fear that none of his collection had suffered. Belial stuffed a handful of painkillers and

Prozac into his mouth and stumbled to his room. He fell into bed and into a fitful sleep. Only moments passed before he awakened to a woman's screams coming from his collection room.

Kay climbed the stairs, calling Dane's name. She arrived at the top of the stairs and pushed open the door to the police station and saw the kerosene heater. Kay was grateful for the warmth after the chill of the tunnel. She opened the door with her mouth open in greeting and froze with horror. The body of Donna Burns was sprawled in naked stillness that only death gives. She began to scream as the flashlight caught the body of Nugent slumped against the bed, a gaping red wound in his chest, his gun clutched in his hand.

Still screaming, Kay bolted down the stairs and tore open the door, dropping the flashlight as she did. As she turned and ran towards the direction of the main building, she heard the shuffling of feet coming towards her. She cried out Dane's name and getting no answer, screamed and fled in the other direction.

Kay saw a faint light in the distance and raced towards the glow. Coming to a half opened door she slipped into the room and saw a scene that could only come from the worst of nightmares. Jar after jar filled the metal shelves on the walls around the room. Some contained triangles of flesh with wisps of hair floating in liquid. Some contained spherical cones floating, with shreds of flesh hanging from them in the liquid. The corpse of a young woman, naked and butchered lay on a metal table. Kay screamed again and fled the horror.

→ Chapter 43

The scream galvanized Belial into action. The short rest and his strong resolve drove the pain from his wounds as he leaped to the door and swiftly ran down the stairs. Someone was in his collection room. The scream belonged to a woman and intuitively, he knew it was the bitch. Exaltation gave him wings and he snatched the lantern from the wall and a knife from the table and rushed into the tunnel. He stopped and listened for the sound of footsteps, poised like a tiger ready to pounce either way. He heard the bitch's steps fading to the left and with a bound was at full speed in pursuit.

Dane was running in the tunnel when he heard the first of Kay's screams. Fear gave him extra strength and he ignored the damage he knew he was doing to his shortened right leg. As he rounded a curve he ran into the back of the giant black and almost fell from the collision. For a moment, he considered Minney as being responsible for Kay's yells for help. This was quickly driven from his mind as he heard Kay scream again. The giant kept plodding forward as Dane ran past him and came to the open door of Drack's house. He stopped long enough to flash his light into the house to ascertain that Kay wasn't there. The flashlight seemed to make the specimens in the jars move. Dane muttered, "Mother of God". He heard Kay scream his name again in the catacombs and he ran towards the sound of her voice.

Kay came to a door that was ajar, and was able to move it wide enough to squeeze through. She went up one flight of stairs and paused to rest and listen.

The footsteps that were following her passed without stopping and pounded by the entrance. Kay began climbing and came to the entrance to the first floor. She tried the door and found it locked. She searched her pockets and found a pack of matches she always kept for June Minney for his cigarettes. She lit a match and her heart sank. The door was marked, Citadel 1. She was on the first floor in the abandoned building called the Citadel.

She had been hoping that the building was one of the houses that was set up for centralizing the patients. She kept climbing and kept trying doors without success at each landing, hoping to find a live telephone so she could call for help.

She was on the fourth floor landing when she heard the entrance door to the tunnel squeal as it was forced open.

Chapter 44

Belial ran for a few minutes, sure he would catch up to the bitch. He paused to catch his breath and listen. There was no sound of footsteps ahead. Was it possible he could have passed her in the darkness? He had to retrace his steps and try the doors on all the buildings he passed. If none were open, then she had to still be ahead of him and he could catch her at his leisure. He retraced his footsteps and tried the two buildings he passed. On the second one, the door was slightly ajar and he put his ear to the opening. He heard footsteps ascending the stairs. He had the bitch trapped. Snarling, he pushed the door wide open, the scream of the rusty hinges breaking the silence of the darkened building.

Dane heard the squeal of the door to the Citadel and tried to move faster. His lungs burned with the additional effort and from the stagnant air of the tunnel. Coming to the open door, he entered the building and leaned on the railing on the stairway for a moment to catch his breath. He could hear steps, just a floor or two ahead of him.

———————————

Kay heard the steps behind her and kept running up the stairs, blessing the runs she and Donna made on the boardwalk. The thought of Donna brought tears to her eyes. She brushed them from her cheeks and kept going up. She finally found a door unlocked on the twelfth floor. Kay pushed against it and was surprised that the wind was so strong up here that she could barely fit through. Fortunately the floor was protected from the snow by the wind and it was blown clear. The floor was icy and she slipped as she closed the door and prayed that her pursuer would keep going to the top.

⟫ Chapter 45

Belial laboriously climbed the last two flights to the tower atop the Citadel. His wound was bleeding again, fueling his rage. He quickly realized that the woman hadn't come this far because he had tried the doors on the last two floors and found them locked. He must have passed the bitch on the way up. But where? He ran down the last two flights trying the doors again. He tried the door on the twelfth floor and found it unlocked. Pushing it open, he just had time to get a glimpse of the bitch when he was struck from behind.

_____

Dane came up the last flight, his lungs burning and his right leg throbbing. He was puzzled to hear footsteps coming down from the top and was just in time to see a figure in white push through the door on the twelfth floor. Summoning a reserve of strength, he took the last steps two at a time.

The figure had halted just outside the door and pulled a huge knife from the side pockets of the white coat he was wearing.

_____

Kay started to back from the figure, and relieved to see who it was and stopped, "Doctor----," she began to say when she saw Belial draw the knife from her pocket. Just then, Dane came hurtling through the door and leaped on the doctor's back.

Belial turned and threw Dane from his back, snarling, "All right, you first," and raised the blade.

As Dane poised to leap at the killer, his foot slipped on the icy roof. As Belial swung his blade at Dane's throat, Kay slammed into him from behind. The blade came down in a shining arc and caught Dane across his out flung arm. Belial, trying to catch his balance, never saw the thrust completed, and thinking the blow had struck home, turned to Kay.

"Now you bitch, I'm going to inflict pain on you that this pit has never experienced."

Belial saw Kay's eyes widen, staring at something behind his back. A powerful arm grabbed his knife hand and twisting, snapped his arm with a terrible crack. Belial felt himself being lifted high in the air and thrown out into the blizzard. As his body flew down, Drack screamed as he felt Belial leave his body. Jim Farkis also screamed as Drack fled too. Farkis fell until he was halted with a terrible tearing pain. His body writhed and twisted trying to get free from the agony, all the while hearing the laughter of his mother. The impassive face of the statue of the knight looked out to sea ignoring the body impaled on his sword.

⇒ Chapter 46

Kay ran to Dane who was attempting to get up. The shock of the stab wound left him disoriented, "Let me and June get you inside and get help. You're bleeding terribly."

Minney picked Dane up as easily as though holding a child and Kay ran to the door and held it open as the big man carried Dane into the Citadel. When Minney laid Jim down out of the wind, Kay opened his parka to look at the wound, the portable phone fell out, "My god! You had this all the time and didn't call for help?"

"In all the excitement, I forgot I had it."

Kay called the command post and was relieved to hear the calm voice of Dr. Younger, "Dr. Younger. we need medical help immediately at the twelfth floor of the Citadel. Jim has been stabbed and is bleeding awfully hard."

"What's happened?"

"Jesus, Doctor! We don't have time for a game of twenty questions. We need a medical doctor with a complete surgical kit. Have two of your biggest aides bring stretchers and blankets along with some guards."

"They'll be there in five minutes."

Kay took of her jacket and removed the sweater underneath. She had Minney tear it into strips and wrapped it as tightly as she could around the slash. The wound ran from elbow to shoulder. The temporary bandage seemed to have slowed the bleeding but Dane was drifting in and out of consciousness. Kay thought an eternity had passed as she sat cradling Danes head. She sobbed with relief as a group of men led be Dr. Kenny and Dr. Younger came charging up the stairs. Dr. Kenny immediately attended to Jim's wound, "Stop worrying Kay, he's lost a lot of blood, but he'll live."

Dane said in a weak voice, "What happened to Farkis?

The last thing I remember is Minney tossing her off the roof."

The whole party stopped what they were doing and Dr. Younger said, "Dr. Farkis? What's she got to do with this?"

Dane said weakly, "She's the killer we've had running loose on the hospital."

One of Dane's uniformed guards came back from peering over the roof, "Mr. Dane, there's a body impaled on one of the statues two floors down."

Dane looked up, "Take two men and go down and see if you can get her loose and bring her to the morgue."

Kay said, "Stop talking," turning to Dr. Younger, "She has a basement room in her house off the tunnels and there's a body on a table just inside the door." Kay shuddered, "The shelves on the walls are loaded with jars filled with a horrible collection."

Dane said, "Put a guard on the house from the tunnel entrance until we can get some help in here."

Dr. Younger looked puzzled, "Why not let Sergeant Nugent take care of that? He knows what to do."

Dane and Kay looked at each other, "He and Mrs. Burns are dead. Farkis killed them in my office."

Before a horrified Younger could ask any more questions, one of Dane's men came running up the stairs shouting, "Dr. Farkis ain't no woman, she's a he!"

With that, due to the combination of lost blood and the pain killer Dr. Kenny gave him, Dane fell into unconsciousness.

→ Chapter 47

Kay, Dane, Dicks and Doctors Younger and Abbott were sitting around a table in the cafeteria drinking coffee. They were watching a television reporter spouting inane drivel about the murders at the hospital until Dr. Abbott got up and turned the set off.

Dane's wound had healed, although his arm was still in a sling. Three weeks had gone by and most of the roads on the Island were open, with only a few side streets still clogged with snow and abandoned cars. The president declared Long Island a disaster area and sent troops from the army corps of engineers to help. The roads in the hospital were all clear and the patients returned to their respective wards.

Dane, "All right, let's hear it. You must have the whole story by now. Who was he?"

"He was a kid from the boonies in New Jersey. I mean the real boonies. Old families that were in the area since revolutionary war times. These people were practically a race of their own. They intermarried and had more than their share of mentally unbalanced offspring. Jim Farkis and his family belonged to a witch's coven that was headed by his mother. He had a twin sister who was murdered along with his mother by an uncle. At least, that's what the cops thought then."

Kay interrupted, "Why don't you think that the uncle wasn't the killer?"

"Because, from the records that were sent me by the Jersey troopers, the wounds on the bodies are pretty much the same as the ones we're finding on the victims here."

Dane asked, "Why did he hide his sex all these years?"

"He and his sister were identical twins. When he showed up at the constable's house the night of the murder, he had dressed in his sister's clothes. Besides the murders of his family, the farmers in the area had a battle with the coven and twenty people burned to death in a fire. The authorities had their hands full and didn't dig too deeply."

"My God! But why pose as his sister."

Dr. Younger spoke up, "He probably had a mother fixation and didn't want to admit that he killed her. Turning himself into his sister freed him of the guilt."

"How the hell did he keep his secret through the years?"

"Easy. He was a loner all his life. The only ones who would have caught on were the people in the town where he grew up. Farkis had sliced the vagina from his sister's body. That's probably where he got started on his collection theme. The medical examiner probably didn't look too closely at the name tag on his sister's body, so he was home free. He was a small town Medical Examiner who had twenty some other bodies from the coven to examine. The mistake just slipped through."

"He was one sick bastard. When I think of those jars in the basement of his house------. Why?"

Dicks answered Dane, "Every motivation is uncertain at best, but a lot of these "collectors" do this because of anger, sex or as in Farkis' case, I believe as a reminder of his mother and sister."

Dicks asked, "No offense Doctor, but how the hell could she, or he, escape detection all these years? I mean, he was surrounded by trained psychiatrists and had to exhibit some abnormality that one of you had to catch."

"No offense taken. First, you have to remember that we had too few doctors to handle all the patients that were crowded into the hospital. We were busy looking at patients and didn't have time to look at our colleagues."

Dane said, "I can remember my first look at him and remarking to Kay that I thought he was off the wall."

Abbott shrugged, "A lot of our doctors have peculiar mannerisms. It's something that comes with the territory."

Dicks, "I've been involved in a couple of dozen murder cases. The ones where the defense was an insanity plea always had two psychiatrists, one for the prosecution and one for the defense. It was as though they were talking about two different people. They never agreed."

Dr. Abbott, "What it comes down to is that, simply stated, we really don't have all the answers. Many an intelligent criminal with access to a prison library can pick up enough insane mannerisms that will fool any psychiatrist."

"Then in all probability, Farkis would have been judged insane and committed to the very hospital he worked as a doctor."

Dr. Abbott answered, "Not here. It looks as though Farkis hammered the last nail in the coffin known as Queens Park. The final plans are in effect to begin closing the institution. It will take a couple of years but it's going to happen."

"What will happen to the patients?

"Most will be turned out into the street. The violent ones will be transferred to the West Slip Hospital on the other side of the Island."

Dane said thoughtfully, "Then that will make the State an accomplice in every crime the released patients commit and every poor bastard like June Minney who gets killed walking on one of our parkways.

———————————

In the basement of the administration of the West Islip Psychiatric Hospital, a patient was unloading boxes of files from Queens Park Hospital. He dropped one of the boxes and files were scattered all over the floor. Cursing, the patient began picking up the files. One was open and the papers opened to view and caught his attention. He began to read the file and as he did, a strange smile came over his face and he began to hum as he replaced the file in its box.

The file read, LEW THOMAS.

Printed in the United States
34161LVS00005B/169-174

9 781420 854398